THE APPEARANCE of a young storyteller with a unique fictional voice is cause for celebration. Yann Martel's title story won the 1991 Journey Prize, and was included in the 1991-92 Pushcart Prize Anthology. The intensely human tragedy that lies at its heart is told with a spare, careful elegance that resonates long after it has ended—and is matched through all the stories by an original and dazzling freshness.

"Yann Martel's new, strong voice weaves together our smallest anxieties and memories with the sentences and executions passed upon all of us by war, crime, and life. AIDS is blended into the lunacy of history. Violins into the Vietnam War. Variations on a warden's letter to the mother of a son he has just hanged are laid out as in a manual of etiquette. Martel has that rare talent of making fiction true and thus painful yet compelling."
     – John Ralston Saul

"'The Facts behind the Helsinki Roccamatios' is a story of extreme youth and death, and I find it hard to describe just how moving it is.... When I finished reading it, I telephoned a friend, wanting company, but found that I was incoherent; I simply couldn't tell her what had happened to me.... It is one of the strange things about art that what devastates us also in some way heals us, or at least leads us to where we need to go."
     – Merna Summers, *Canadian Forum*

YANN MARTEL was born in 1963 in Salamanca, Spain, the son of peripatetic diplomats. He has lived in Alaska, British Columbia, Costa Rica, France, Mexico, and Ontario where he studied philosophy at Trent University. He now lives in Montreal.

The Facts behind the Helsinki Roccamatios

and other stories

Yann Martel

Alfred A. Knopf Canada

PUBLISHED BY ALFRED A. KNOPF CANADA

Copyright © 1993 by Yann Martel

Published in Canada by Alfred A. Knopf Canada, Toronto, and
simultaneously in Great Britain by Faber and Faber, London. All rights
reserved under International and Pan-American Copyright Conventions.
Distributed by Random House of Canada Limited, Toronto

Canadian Cataloguing in Publication Data

Martel, Yann
The facts behind the Helsinki Roccamatios and other stories

ISBN 0-394-22732-8

I. Title.

PS 8576.A78F3 1993   C813'.54   C92-095537-1
PR9199.3.M378F3 1993

The author would like to thank John Ralston Saul, Connie Rooke and
Ellen Seligman for their help and encouragement.

Some of the facts behind the Helsinki Roccamatios are based on
information drawn from the following invaluable sources: *Canada's
Illustrated Heritage* (ed. Toivo Kiil); *The Canadian Encyclopedia*
(ed. James H. Marsh); *Encyclopaedia Britannica*; and *An Encyclopedia
of World History* (ed. William L. Langer).

Three of these stories have previously appeared in slightly different form:
"The Facts behind the Helsinki Roccamatios" and "The Time I Heard The
Private Donald J. Rankin String Concerto" in *The Malahat Review*, and
"Manners of Dying" in *STORY*.

Design: John Pylypczuk and Diti Katona / Concrete
Author photo: Anthony Wolfe

First Edition
Printed and bound in Canada

Toronto, New York, London, Sydney, Auckland

The Facts behind the Helsinki Roccamatios

and other stories

Contents

The Facts behind the Helsinki Roccamatios

pour J. G.

I hadn't known Paul for very long. We had met at Trent University in Peterborough in the fall of 1987. I had worked and travelled around and I was older than him, twenty-four and in fourth year. He had just turned nineteen and was entering first year. At the beginning of the year at Trent, some senior students introduce the first-years to the university. There are no pranks or anything like that; the seniors are there to be helpful. They're called "amigas" and the first-years "amigees", which shows you how much Spanish they speak in Peterborough. I was an amiga and most of my amigees struck me as good-humoured, eager children. But Paul had a laid-back, intelligent curiosity and a skeptical turn of mind that I liked. And it happened that because of our parents' jobs we had both lived in Mexico City for a few years when we were kids. The two of us clicked and we became good friends. We did things together and talked all the time. Because I was older and I had seen more things, I would usually fall into the role of the wise old guru and Paul into that of the young disciple. But then he would say something that threw my pompousness right into my face and we would laugh and break from these roles.

Then, hardly into second term, Paul fell ill. Already at Christmas he had had a fever, and ever since then he had been carrying this cough around. If he moved suddenly, if he sat down or got up too quickly, for example, he would erupt into a dry, hacking cough. Initially, he, we, thought nothing of it. The cold, the dryness of the air—it was something to do with that.

But slowly things got worse. Now I recall signs that I didn't think twice about at the time. He complained once of diarrhea. He seemed less energetic. One day we were climbing the stairs to the library, hardly twenty-five steps, and when we reached the top, we stopped. I remember realizing that the only reason we had stopped was because Paul wanted to rest. He was out of breath. And he was never finishing his meals, either, and seemed to be losing weight. It was hard to tell, what with the heavy winter sweaters and all, but I'm certain that his frame had been stockier. Finally, when he was getting

winded at the smallest effort, it became clear that something was wrong. We talked about it—nearly casually,
you must understand—and I played doctor and said,
"Hum. Out of breath, cough, weight loss, tiredness—
Paul, you have pneumonia." I was joking, of course.
Ironically, that's in fact what he had. It's called *Pneumocystis carinii pneumonia*, PCP to intimates. Late in February, Paul left for Toronto to see his family doctor.

Eight months later he was dead.

AIDS. He said it to me over the phone in this strange,
removed voice. He had been gone for a week. He had just
got back from the hospital, he told me. I reeled. AIDS.
AIDS! My first thoughts were for myself. Had I ever
drunk out of his glass? Used his soap? Come into contact
with his blood? I tried to remember if he had ever cut
himself in my presence. Or scratched me accidentally.
Then I thought of him. I thought of sex, of homosexuality. But Paul wasn't gay. I mean, he had never told me so
outright, but I knew him well enough and I had never
detected the least ambivalence. That wasn't it, anyway.
Four years ago, when he was fifteen, he had gone to
Jamaica on holiday with his parents. They had had a car
accident and Paul had been gashed in the left thigh. He
had lost a quantity of blood and had received a transfusion at the local hospital. Six witnesses of the accident
had come along to volunteer blood. Three were of the
right blood group. Several phone calls and a little
research turned up the fact that one of the three had died
two years later of toxoplasmic cerebral lesions while

being treated for pneumonia, a suspicious combination.

I went to visit Paul that weekend at his home in Rosedale. I didn't want to—it was he who asked; I wanted to block the whole thing off; I asked, this was my excuse, if he was sure his parents cared for a visitor—but he insisted that I come. And I did, I came through. And I was right. Because what hurt most that first weekend was not Paul, but Paul's family.

After learning how he had probably caught the virus, Paul's father didn't utter a syllable for three days. Then, early one morning, he fetched the tool kit in the basement, stepped out to the driveway and destroyed the family car. Because he had been the driver when they had had the accident; even though it hadn't been his fault and it had been in another car, a rented car. He took a hammer and shattered all the windows and lights and then he scrapped and trashed the body and then he banged nails into the tires. Then he siphoned the gasoline from the tank, poured it over and inside the car and set it on fire. The neighbours called the police and the fire department and they rushed to the scene, but when he blurted out why he was doing it, they were very understanding and put the fire out and left without charging him or anything, only asking if he wanted to go to the hospital, which he didn't. So that was the first thing I saw when I walked up to Paul's house—a burnt wreck of a Mercedes covered in dried-out foam.

Paul's father didn't shake my hand when Paul introduced me. He was walking about the living room, trembling and constantly rubbing his face with his hands. Paul's mother was in their bedroom. As a young woman, she had earned an M.A. in linguistics from McGill and she had been a highly ranked amateur tennis player. Paul was very proud of her. That child-rearing and spouse-playing had turned her talents into hobbies nourished in him (though not in her) the faintest resentment against his father, who was a hard-working non-athlete who practised the non-sexy profession of lawyer, corporate at that. Paul's mother was, and is, a very good-looking, nimble-minded, energetic woman. Paul had shown me pictures of her. But here she was, sitting on the edge of the bed, looking like a balloon that has become deflated and wrinkled. As though all the vitality had been drained out of her. She was staring in mid-air and she was slowly and methodically chewing her hangnails till they bled. When I brought out my hand, she just looked at it, baffled, and I quickly pulled it back. Paul's sister, Jennifer, who was twenty-one and an architecture student at the University of Toronto, was the most normally hysterical. Her eyes were red, her face was puffy—she looked terrible. I don't mean to be grimly funny, but even George H., the family Labrador, was grief-stricken. He had squeezed himself under the living-room sofa, wouldn't budge and was whining all the time.

Confirmation of the verdict had come on Tuesday and since then (it was Friday) none of them, George H. included, had eaten a particle of food. The whole family structure had fallen apart. Paul's father, who after working several years with the International Monetary Fund had joined a Toronto law firm, and his mother, who was a part-time librarian in addition to a very active NDP militant, hadn't gone to work and Jennifer hadn't gone to school, had hardly even left her room. They slept, when they slept, fully dressed and wherever they happened to be. One morning I found Paul's father slouched on the living-room floor.

In the middle of it all was Paul, who wasn't reacting. He introduced me to his family the way an asylum director would showcase his most deranged inmates. He was frightened dumb. Only on the fourth day of my stay did he start to react. He couldn't understand what was happening to him. He knew it was awful, but he couldn't grasp it. He spoke of his condition as if it were a theoretical abstraction, a moot point of philosophy. He would say, "I'm going to die," as he might say, "The game was a tie." Death was just a word.

I had meant to stay for the weekend only—there was school—but I ended up staying for two weeks. I did a lot of house-cleaning and cooking during that time. The family didn't seem to notice or care, but that was all right. Paul helped me, and he liked that because it gave him something to think about. We had the car towed away, we replaced the phones that Paul's father had destroyed, we cleaned the house spotlessly from top to bottom, we walked George H. and gave him a good bath (George H. because Paul really liked the Beatles and it was Paul who brought George into the band, and when Paul was a kid he liked to say to himself when he was walking the dog or, rather, when the dog was walking him, since George H. was an affectionate but generally ill-mannered beast, he liked to say to himself, "At this very moment, unbeknown to anyone, absolutely in-cog-*nee-to*, Beatle Paul and Beatle George are walking the streets of Rosedale," and he would dream about what it would be like to sing "Help!" in Shea Stadium or something like that) and we nudged the family into eating. I say "we" and "Paul helped"— what I mean is, I did everything in his presence. Drugs called dapsone and trimethoprim were overcoming Paul's pneumonia, but he was still weak and out of breath. He moved about like an old man, slowly and conscious of every exertion. I spent myself without respite.

It took the family a while to break out of its daze. During the course of Paul's illness, I noticed three states they would go through. In the first, common in the beginning, at home, when the pain was too close, they would isolate themselves from each other and do their thing: Paul's father would destroy something sturdy, like a table or a major appliance; Paul's mother would sit on the edge of her bed and make her hangnails bleed; Jennifer would cry in her bedroom; and George H. would hide under the sofa and whine. In the second, later on, at the hospital mostly, they would come together and sit on the bed beside Paul and they would talk and sob and encourage each other and whisper. And finally, in the third, they would display what I suppose you could call normality, an ability to get through the day as if death didn't exist, a calm, somewhat numb face of courage that, because it was required every single day, became both heroic and ordinary. The family went through these states over the course of several months, or in an hour.

I'm not going to talk about what AIDS does to a human body. Imagine it very bad—and then make it worse. Look up in the dictionary the word "flesh"—it's a healthy, pink word—and then look up the word "melt".

Anyway, that's not the worst of it. The worst of it is the resistance put up, the I'm-not-going-to-die virus. It's the one that kills the most people because it kills the living, the ones who surround and love the dying. That virus infected me early on. I remember the day precisely. Paul was in the hospital. He was eating his supper, eating his whole supper, eating every morsel though he wasn't at all hungry. I watched him as he carefully pricked every carrot and every pea and as he consciously masticated every mouthful before swallowing. "It will help my body fight. Every little bit counts"—I could see this was what he was thinking. It was written all over his face, all over his body, all over the walls. I wanted to scream, scream, "You're going to die, Paul, *DIE!* Like people in cemeteries, you know." Except that "death" was now a tacitly forbidden word. So I just sat there, my face emptied of any expression, this painful anger roiling me up inside. My condition got much worse every time I saw Paul shave. You see, though Paul was nineteen, all he had were a few downy whiskers on his chin. Still, he began to shave as though he'd become as hairy as a werewolf. Every single day he would lather up his face with a mountain of shaving cream and would scrape it off with a Bic razor. That's the image that rips through me: a vacillatingly healthy Paul standing in front of a mirror turning his head this way and that, pulling his skin here and there, meticulously doing something that was utterly, utterly useless.

I completely botched my academic year. I was skipping lectures and seminars all the time. I was incoherently angry at everything and everybody and I didn't, couldn't, write any essays. I developed a loathing for Canada, Canadians and things Canadian, a loathing which still hasn't left me entirely. This country reeked of insipidity, comfort and insularity. Canadians were up to their necks in materialism and from the neck above it was all American television. Nowhere could I see idealism or transcendentalism, a concern for something come what may. There was nothing but a deadening, flavourless realism. It became my instinct to despise Canadian politicians, starting with the Governor General, then the Prime Minister and then working my way down. Bill Domm, the Member of Parliament for Peterborough, the opaque dimwit who led the fight to re-establish the death penalty and to block the adoption of the metric system, struck me as typical excrement of the Canadian mediocratic system. Canada's policy on Central America, on native issues, on the environment, on Reagan, on everything, made my stomach turn. Really, there was nothing about this country that I liked.

Yes, I know—as if political activism or Gandhi-like asceticism could do anything about AIDS.

One day in a philosophy seminar—that was my major—I was doing a presentation on Hegel's philosophy of history. The professor, a highly intelligent and considerate man, interrupted me and asked me to elucidate a point he hadn't understood. I was silent for a second—I was confused; I couldn't make sense of anything; I looked about the cosy, book-filled office where we were having our seminar—and then I exploded. I screamed, got up, projected the hefty Hegel brick through the closed window and then I stormed out of the office, slamming the door as hard as I could and, for good measure, kicking in two of its nicely sculptured panels.

I tried to withdraw from Trent, but I missed the deadline. I appealed, and appeared in front of a committee, the Committee on Undergraduate Standings and Petitions, CUSP they call it. My grounds for withdrawing were Paul, but when the chairman of CUSP prodded me and asked me in a glib little voice what exactly I meant by "emotional distress", I looked at him and I decided that I wasn't going to decorticate Paul's agony for him. But I didn't make a scene. I just stood up, walked out without saying a word and quietly shut the door behind me.

So I failed my year. But I didn't care and I don't care. I hung around Peterborough, a nice place to hang around.

But what I really want to tell you about, the purpose of this story, is the Roccamatio family of Helsinki. That's not Paul's family, of course. His last name was Atsea. Nor is it my family.

You see, Paul spent months in the hospital. When his condition was stable he came home, but mostly I remember him at the hospital. The structure of his illnesses, tests and treatments became the structure of his life. Against my will, I became familiar with words like azidothymidine, alpha interferon, domipramine, nitrazepam. (When you're with people who are really sick—AIDS or cancer or whatever—you discover what a chimera science can be.)

I would visit Paul. I didn't manage to get a job in Toronto, but in the spring I got one in nearby Oshawa. I was coming in to Toronto to see Paul once, twice a week, often on weekends too, and I was calling him all the time. When I visited, if he was strong enough, we would go to a movie or a play or for a walk, but generally we just sat about. But when you're between four walls and neither of you wants to watch television and the papers have been read aloud and you're sick of playing cards and chess and Trivial Pursuit and you can't always be talking about *it* and *its* progress, you run out of things to do. Which in a way was fine. Neither Paul nor I minded just sitting there, listening to quiet music, lost in our own thoughts.

Except that I started feeling that time was running out and we had to do something. I don't mean put on togas and ruminate philosophically about life, death, reality and God. We had done all that in first term, before we even knew he was sick. That's the basic staple of undergraduate life. What else is there to talk about when you've decided one night to stay up till sunrise? Or when he's just read Descartes or Berkeley for the first time? And anyway, Paul was nineteen. What are you at nineteen? You're a blank page. You're all hopes and dreams and uncertainties, you're all future and little philosophy. What I meant was that, between the two of us, we had to do something that would go beyond life and death and dying of AIDS, something that would make sense of nonsense.

So what I thought Paul and I would do—the idea came to me on a GO Transit bus back to Oshawa; what an excellent way of destroying void, I thought—was create something with our imaginations, a story that we would tell each other each time we were together.

I gave it a good thinking. I had plenty of time to think on my job; I was a gardener for the municipality of Oshawa, and I spent my time mowing lawns, tending flower beds and clipping shrubbery. It would be a series of stories. A bit like Boccaccio's *Decameron* except that, instead of being ten people, we would be two. And it wouldn't last ten days, but indefinitely. Nor would it be discrete, unrelated stories. I wanted continuity, something that would develop and meander. No, come to think of it, it wouldn't be like the *Decameron*. Ten healthy people fleeing a world dying of the Black Death who tell each other saucy little stories only to pass the time—that structure never struck me as quite right. Our situation would be very different. We the storytellers would be the sick this time, fleeing a healthy world. And we would be telling each other stories not to forget the world, but to remember it, to re-create it. Yes, to re-create it.

The more I thought about the idea, the more I liked it. I would have to be well prepared so that I could carry the story all by myself when Paul was too weak or depressed. And when he was up to it, I would have to be a firm guide and not let it slide into autobiography. It would be important, too, that I convince him that he had no choice, that he couldn't take it as a game or something on the same level as watching a movie or talking about politics. He would have to see that everything else was useless, even his desperate existential thoughts that did nothing but frighten him. Only the imaginary must matter.

But the imaginary doesn't spring from nothing. If our story was to have any stamina, any breadth and depth, if it was to avoid both true life and irrelevant fantasy, it would need a structure, a guideline of sorts, some curb along which we could tap our white canes. As I mowed Oshawa lawns, I racked my brains trying to think of just such a structure. The story would be about a family. A large family, to allow diverse yet related stories. And contemporary and Western, so that cultural references would be easy. But I needed something firmer, something that would both restrict and inspire us.

Finally, while clipping a hedgerow, I hit upon it: we would use the history of the twentieth century. Not that the story would start in 1901 and progress up to 1987.

That wouldn't be much of a blueprint; rather, we would use one event of each year as a metaphorical guideline. The twentieth century would be our mould. It would be a story in eighty-seven episodes, each echoing an event of one year of the century.

To have figured out what to make of my time with Paul electrified me. I was bursting with ideas. Nothing struck me as more worthwhile than making the trip from Oshawa to Toronto—commuting, imagine; that dull, work-related chore—to invent stories with Paul.

I explained it carefully to him. It was at the hospital. He was undergoing tests.

"I don't get it," he replied. "What do you mean by 'metaphorical guideline'? Will the story start in 1901?"

"No, it'll start nowadays. The historical events we choose will just be a parallel, something to guide us in making up our stories. The way a builder uses an architect's plans. Even better: like Homer's *Odyssey* for Joyce's *Ulysses*."

"I've never read the book."

"Nor have I. The point is, the novel takes place in Dublin in 1906 but it's named after an ancient Greek epic. Joyce uses the ten years' wandering of Ulysses after the Trojan War as a parallel for his story in Dublin. His story is a metaphorical transformation of the Odyssey."

"Why don't we just read the book aloud, since we've never read it?"

"Because we don't want to be spectators, Paul."

"Oh."

He seemed skeptical, he was tired, but I insisted. I even got a touch annoyed—I didn't use the D word but it was in the air—and he started to cry. I apologized immediately. Yes, we would read *Ulysses* aloud, what a good idea, and then, why not, *War and Peace*.

But when I had left his room, when I had nearly stepped into the elevator—a long scream exploded in the corridor.

"Helllllllllllsinnnnnnnnnnnkiiiiiiiiiiiiiiiiiiiiii!"

I smiled. You see, Paul and I were on the same wavelength. We were young and the young can be radical. We're not encrusted with habits and traditions. If we catch ourselves in time, we can start all over.

So—the story would take place in Helsinki. It was a good choice. Neither of us had been there and we knew next to nothing about the city. I returned to Paul's room. His face was still red.

"The video machine will have to go," he said. Hip, hip, hurray! What about the name of the family? He pouted his lips and narrowed his eyes. Then he expelled the word "Roccamatio". *What?* "Roccamatio—Raw-ka-mah-tee-o." I wasn't very keen about that one. Not very realistic. I would have chosen a more Scandinavian-sounding name, like Karlson or Harviki. But Paul insisted: the Roccamatios were a Finnish family of Italian extraction. So be it. The Helsinki Roccamatios were located and baptized. We agreed on the rules: I would be the judge of what was fictionally acceptable; transparent biography was forbidden; the story would take place nowadays, in the 1980s; the episodes would resemble events of our choosing from each consecutive year of the twentieth century; each episode would take into account what had taken place in previous ones and would be related in one sitting; we would alternate in narrating the story. We agreed that the basic facts about Helsinki were: one, it was an important port; two, it had a population of a million inhabitants; three, it was in all ways the capital of Finland—political, commercial, industrial, cultural, etc.; and four, it had a small but significant Swedish-speaking minority. Finally, we agreed that the Roccamatios would be a secret between the two of us.

We decided that after a period of thinking about it and doing research I would start with the first episode. I brought Paul some paper, a pen and a thick, three-volume work called *A History of the 20th Century*. His father took the video machine away, set a small bookcase with wheels beside his bed and filled it with all thirty volumes of *Encyclopaedia Britannica*.

Now, understand that you're not going to hear the story of the Helsinki Roccamatios. Certain intimacies shouldn't be aired. At most they should be known to exist. The telling of the story of the Roccamatios was difficult, especially as the years went by. We started brave and strong, arguing about facts and events, interrupting each other, surprising ourselves with our inventiveness— but it's so tiring re-creating the world when you're not in the peak of health. Paul would be not so much unwilling—he would still redirect me or correct me with a word or a scowl—as unable. Even listening became tiring.

The story of the Helsinki Roccamatios was often whispered. And it wasn't whispered to you.

Of these AIDS years, all I have kept—outside my head—is this record:

The Facts behind the Helsinki Roccamatios

1901—After a reign of sixty-four years, Queen Victoria dies. Her reign has witnessed a period of incredible industrial expansion and increasing material prosperity. In its own blinkered and delusional way, the Victorian age has been the happiest of all—an age of stability, order, wealth, enlightenment and hope. Science and technology are new and triumphant and Utopia seems at hand.

I begin with an ending, with the death of Sandro Roccamatio, the patriarch of the family. It is dramatic and it allows me to introduce the family members, who are all at the funeral.

1902—Under the forceful leadership of Clifford Sifton, Laurier's Minister of the Interior, the settlement of Canada's west is in full swing. Sifton sends out millions of pamphlets in dozens of languages and strings a net of agents across northern and central

Europe. The shipping lines, having just dumped their Canadian wheat on the Old Continent, bring home the catch. In less than a decade, the population of the Prairies increases by close to a million inhabitants and wheat production jumps fivefold. The origins of the new settlers are myriad: Ukrainian, German, Balkan, Scandinavian, Russian, British, Austrian, American, Polish. It's called "the Canadian miracle".

1903—Orville and Wilbur Wright fly at Kill Devil Hills, North Carolina. Their powered machine, "Flyer I" (now popularly called "Kitty Hawk"), stays in the air for twelve seconds on its first flight, fifty-nine seconds on its fourth and last.

1904—As a direct result of the Dreyfus affair, Prime Minister Emile Combes of France introduces a bill for the complete separation of Church and State. The bill guarantees complete liberty of conscience, removes the State from having any say in the appointment of ecclesiastics or in the payment of their salaries and severs all other connections between Church and State.

A routine to our storytelling has already developed. It's nearly a ceremony. First, and always first, we shake hands every time we meet, like the Europeans. Paul takes pleasure in this, I can tell. Then we small-talk, usually about politics since we're both diligent newspaper readers.

Then, if there's a need, we deal with health and therapy. Finally, after a short pause to collect ourselves, we get on with the Roccamatios.

1905—The German monthly Annalen der Physik publishes papers by Albert Einstein, a twenty-six-year-old German Jew who works as an examiner in a patent office in Bern, Switzerland. The Special Theory of Relativity is born. There is energy everywhere. E = mc², as Einstein puts it.

1906—Tommy Burns defeats Marvin Hart to become the first (and only) Canadian to win the world heavyweight boxing championship. Burns defends his title ten times in thirty-three months, notably knocking out the Irish champion Jem Roche in 1 minute 28 seconds, the shortest heavyweight title defence ever.

Paul is nearly well. He is plagued by minor ills—night sweating here, diarrhea there—and a lack of energy, but it's nothing so dramatic. He is at home; and as he has never been sick before a day in his life, the routine of illness has an exotic appeal. He is started on a program of azidothymidine (AZT) and multivitamins and is going to the hospital several times a week, sometimes staying overnight. He likes the hospital. The omnipotent men and women in white, their scientific jargon, the innumerable tests, the impeccable cleanliness of the place—

they exhaust and reassure him. His mood is good.

We speak of the future, make plans. We speak of travel. I have travelled some, Paul less, mostly with his family, and we both perceive travel as essential to growth, as a state of being, as a metaphor for inner journeying. We hardly speak of Europe—we have touched on the south of France and Iceland, but that's it. We are going to be travellers, not tourists. The travellers will go to North Yemen, will wander the streets of San'a and Hodeida and perhaps chew qat. The travellers will go to India, will get to know the Punjab and Bengal and Uttar Pradesh as they know the backs of their hands, as they will know Mexico again, and Bolivia and Peru, as they will know South Africa and the Philippines and Indonesia. The travellers will travel.

1907—A new strain of wheat, Marquis, is sent out to Indian Head, Saskatchewan, for testing. It is the result of an exhaustive scientific selection process, the credit for which goes to Charles Edwards Saunders, cerealist at the Ottawa Experimental Farm. The new strain's response to Saskatchewan conditions is phenomenal. It is resistant to heavy winds and to disease and it produces high yields that make excellent flour. Most important, it matures early, thus avoiding the damage of frost and greatly extending the areas of Alberta and Saskatchewan where wheat can be grown. By 1920, Marquis will make up 90 per cent of prairie spring wheat, helping make Canada,

already known as a wheat-growing area, one of the
great breadbaskets of the world.

If I'm not distracted by other people and their words, or
by thoughts of food, transportation and the like, I think
of the Roccamatios. They are my mind's natural subject.
I have to find historical events. Then I have to think of
plot and parallel, of the way in which the story will
resemble the historical event, whether in an obvious way
or a subtle way, whether for one symbolic moment (at
the beginning or the end?) or all along. These thoughts
pester me, challenge me, make me go on. I am hardly
aware of Oshawa.

1908—Ernest Thompson Seton, famous author,
naturalist and artist, organizes the Boy Scouts of
Canada. The aim of the organization, like that of the
Girl Guides, founded two years later, is to foster good
citizenship, decent behaviour, love of nature and skill
in various outdoor activities. The Scouts follow a
moral code and are encouraged to perform a daily
good deed. They go camping, swimming, sailing and
hiking. They undertake community service projects.
Their motto is "Be Prepared" and they shake hands
with the left hand.

I had not envisioned the Roccamatios so ambitiously.
Marriages, the runaway daughter, the bitter but liberating
divorce, childbirths, entrepreneurial success, romance,

community leadership—they are a dynamic family. Paul and I go about them briskly. I meant for us to alternate years, but so far they have been more of a co-operative endeavour.

But there are clouds on the horizon. The year 1909 is mine. I see trial and error in my story; Paul, trial and fraud. It's the first time we quibble. And I'm troubled by his story for 1910.

1909—Commander Robert E. Peary, on his third attempt, claims to reach the North Pole. Though generally accepted, the claim is questioned by many because of the inadequacy of his observations and the incredible timetable of travelling he has submitted. Possibly, Peary never reached the Pole.

1910—Japan, increasingly militaristic and expansionist, annexes Korea and begins a program of development and attempted assimilation.

I launch the Roccamatios into Helsinki municipal politics.

1911—A federal election is called in Canada. The dominant issue of the campaign is reciprocity, an arrangement to lower tariffs between Canada and the United States. Liberal Prime Minister Wilfrid Laurier favours reciprocity. Conservative Opposition leader Robert Borden doesn't. Eastern Canadian

*manufacturers cry that such an economic accord will
be the first step in a political takeover. Certain state-
ments by influential Americans—"I hope to see the
day when the American flag will float over every
square foot of the British North American possessions, clear to the North Pole": Champ Clark,
Speaker of the House of Representatives—seem to
justify these fears. Laurier and his Liberals go down
to a resounding defeat. Eight Cabinet ministers lose
their seats and the two parties practically switch
places: the Liberals go from 135 seats to 87, the
Conservatives from 85 to 134. Robert Borden
becomes Prime Minister.*

Paul's moods are changing. I think he is starting to realize
what he's in for. Initially, his pills and injections were a
source of delight. "Here comes health," he probably said
to himself. "I'll beat this." But health seems to elude him
and he is angry about it. He still takes all his medicines
religiously, but they are bitter now, not sweet. In 1912
the Minimum Wage law is passed in England, Roald
Amundsen reaches the South Pole, Ludwig Borchardt
discovers Queen Nefertiti in Egypt. But Paul will have
none of these. His story is nasty.

*1912—After a siege of five hours in Choisy-le-Roy, a
suburb of Paris, Jules Joseph Bonnot, the leader of a
group of anarchists known as* la bande à Bonnot, *is
killed. Bonnot and his gang have been terrorizing*

French society with the ease and nonchalance with which they shoot tellers, guards, passers-by, policemen, dwellers and drivers during their barefaced bank robberies, break-ins and car thefts. In the final attack on his holdout, the police, against a solitary Bonnot, deploy three artillery regiments and at least five police brigades and they use guns, heavy machine guns and dynamite. Bonnot is found, still alive, wrapped in a mattress. He is summarily finished off. There are over 30,000 spectators at the siege.

Durable optimism can be the product of only one thing: reason. Any optimism that is unreasonable is bound to be dashed by reality and result in even more unhappiness. Optimism, therefore, must be girded by reason, must be unshakeably grounded in it, so that pessimism becomes a foolish, short-sighted attitude. What this means—reasonableness being the inglorious, tepid thing it is—is that optimism can arise only from small, nearly ridiculous, but undeniable achievements. In 1913, I put my best foot forward.

1913—G. Sundbank patents the zipper.

Paul is hospitalized. He is having a relapse of *Pneumocystis carinii.* He is put on dapsone and trimethoprim again, but this time he suffers side effects: a fever, a rash all over his neck and chest. And he is amazingly thin; he hardly eats and suffers from intractable diarrhea. He has a tube up his nose. He has Marco Roccamatio have a serious fall-out with his brother Orlando.

> *1914—Austria declares war on Serbia,*
>> *Germany on Russia,*
>> *Germany on France,*
>> *Germany on Belgium,*
>> *Great Britain (and therefore, nearly automatically, Canada, India, Australia, New Zealand, South Africa and Newfoundland) on Germany,*
>> *Montenegro on Austria,*
>> *Austria on Russia,*
>> *Serbia on Germany,*
>> *Montenegro on Germany,*
>> *France on Austria,*
>> *Great Britain on Austria,*
>> *Japan on Germany,*
>> *Japan on Austria,*
>> *Austria on Belgium,*
>> *Russia on Turkey,*
>> *Serbia on Turkey,*
>> *Great Britain on Turkey,*
>> *France on Turkey,*
>> *Egypt on Turkey.*

I tell Paul 1914 was the year Aspirin was commercialized, and wouldn't it make a more pleasant story?

"Your history is biased," he replies.

"So is yours," I shoot back.

"But mine is the correct bias."

"How do you know?"

"Because it accounts for the future."

I can't understand it. I have read of people who have AIDS who live for years. Yet week by week Paul is getting thinner and weaker. He is receiving treatments, yes, but they don't seem to be doing much, except for his pneumonia. Anyway, he doesn't seem to have any particular illness, just a wasting away. I ask Science about it, nearly complain about it: I ask a doctor who is standing in a doorway. He has his eyes closed and he is slowly rubbing them. He listens to my litany without saying a word—he is a big man and his eyes are a bit red—and then he doesn't say anything and finally after several seconds he says, in a low, measured voice, "We're—doing—our—best."

It is my turn. But I must be careful. I must neither give in to Paul nor ignore him. I must steer between total abstraction and grim reality. I would like Einstein again, the announcement of his *General* Theory of Relativity this time, but a reminder that the universe is created anew would not please Paul. Yet I refuse to invoke further declarations of war. I tread carefully. I go for the ambiguous.

1915—Alfred Wegener, in Die Entstehung der Kontinente und Ozeane, *gives the classic expression of the controversial theory of continental drift.*

"Continental drift? *Drift?*" Paul smiles. He likes my story too.

> *1916—Germany declares war on Portugal,*
> *Austria on Portugal,*
> *Romania on Austria,*
> *Italy on Germany,*
> *Germany on Romania,*
> *Turkey on Romania,*
> *Bulgaria on Romania.*

More tests. Paul has something called cytomegalovirus, which may account for his diarrhea and his general weakness. It's a highly disseminating infection, could affect his eyes, liver, lungs, gastrointestinal tract, spinal cord, brain, anywhere. There's nothing to be done; no effective therapy exists. Paul is speechlessly depressed. I give in to him.

> *1917—The United States declares war on Germany,*
> *Panama on Germany,*
> *Cuba on Germany,*
> *Bolivia severs relations with Germany,*
> *Turkey with the United States,*
> *Greece declares war on Austria, Bulgaria,*
> *   Germany and Turkey,*
> *Siam on Germany and Austria,*
> *Liberia on Germany,*
> *China on Germany and Austria,*

Peru severs relations with Germany,
Uruguay with Germany,
Brazil declares war on Germany,
the United States on Austria,
Ecuador severs relations with Germany,
Panama declares war on Austria,
Cuba on Austria.

In 1918, Paul wants to use further declarations of war—Guatemala declared war on Germany; Nicaragua on Germany and Austria; Costa Rica on Germany; Haiti on Germany; Honduras on Germany—but for the first time I use my power of veto and declare these fictionally unacceptable. Nor do I accept the publication of Oswald Spengler's *The Decline of the West*, in which Spengler gives a cyclical interpretation of history and forecasts as inevitable the eclipse of Western civilization. Enough is enough, I tell Paul. There is hope. The sun still shines. Paul is angry at me but he is tired and submits. I think he was expecting my censure, for he surprises me with a curious event and a fully prepared Roccamatio story.

1918—After an extensive study of the distribution of globular clusters and cepheid and RR Lyrae variable stars, Harlow Shapley increases the estimated size of our galaxy by about ten times. He envisions it as a flattened, lens-shaped system of stars in which our solar system occupies a position far away—some 30,000 light-years—from the centre.

"Isn't it grand," I say.

"Aren't we lonely," he replies.

His story—of Orlando, of alcoholism—is ugly.

1919—John Alcock and Arthur Brown make the first nonstop airplane crossing of the Atlantic. Taking off from St. John's, Newfoundland, they land in a bog near Clifden, County Galway, Ireland, 16 hours and 12 minutes later.

"This AZT is exhausting," says Paul. He is anemic because of it and receives blood transfusions regularly.

In 1920, I forbid the publication of Freud's *Beyond the Pleasure Principle*, in which Freud concludes that the fundamental aim of all instincts is to revert to an earlier state, a notion that is soon popularized as the "death wish". Paul changes historical events while keeping the same Roccamatio story.

1920—With Tristan Tzara at the helm, Dada triumphs.

Over the phone, Paul tells me he is developing Kaposi's sarcoma. He has purple, blue lesions on his feet and ankles. Not many, but they are there. The doctors have zeroed in on them. He will be put on alpha interferon. He will have radiation therapy. Paul's voice is shaky. But we agree, we strongly agree, that radiation therapy has been found to be successful against localized Kaposi's sarcoma, and he's only got it on his skin, in fact, only on his feet, and it doesn't hurt and at least his lungs are fine. I promise to come by the hospital.

Paul is quiet. He is in his usual, favourite position: lying on his back at a very specific angle against a carefully arranged pyramid of three pillows.

1921—Frederick Banting, Charles Best, Bert Collip and John Macleod discover the long-sought internal secretion of the pancreas. They call it insulin. It is immediately and spectacularly effective as a therapy for diabetes. Banting, the most famous of the discoverers though actually the least skilled as a scientist, is an accomplished amateur painter. In his style, he is clearly influenced by his good friend the painter A.Y. Jackson.

I have just started my story when Paul interrupts me.

"In 1921 Albert Camus died in a car crash."

He doesn't say anything more. I continue. Until he interrupts me once again.

"In 1921 Albert Camus died in a car crash."

"Paul. He didn't. Camus died in 1960."

"In 1921 Albert Camus died in a car crash. He was in the car, a Facel-Vega—never heard of it, have you? It was a small series, French copy of a Chrysler, not very road-tested. He was in the car with Michel and Janine Gallimard and their daughter Anne."

"Paul, Albert Camus died in 1960."

"In 1921 Camus was beside Michel Gallimard, who was driving. They were returning to Paris from Loumarin, in the Lubéron, where Camus had bought a beautiful white house with his Nobel money. Near a village called Villeblevin, the road was —"

"Paul, stop it. It's my turn."

"—the road was straight and dry and empty. Along the road were trees, plane trees. The French like plane trees. Suddenly —"

"Paul, I said it was in 1960. *1960!*"

"In 1921, suddenly—an axle that broke? a wheel that blocked?—for no reason, the car—"

"Paul, you're not following the rules, you're chea—"

"—THE CAR SLID AND HIT ONE TREE AND THEN ANOTHER. Albert Camus was crushed, quite crushed. Body all mangled, organs squeezed out. As for Michel Gallimard, the steering shaft went through his fucking chest and pinned him like a butter—"

"STOP IT."

"—like a butterfly. Janine and Anne Gallimard survived. To tell the tale. In fact, they were hardly injured."

"In 1921 Banting, Best, Collip and Macleod discovered the long-sought internal secretion of the pan—"

"In 1921 the atomic bomb was dropped on Hiroshima."

"In 1921 Banting, Best, Collip and Macleod discovered the long-sought—"

"IN 1921 THE ATOMIC BOMB WAS—"

"THEY CALLED IT INSULIN AND IT WAS SPECTACULARLY EFFECTIVE—"

"THE A-BOMB WAS —"

"IT WAS SPECTACULARLY EFFECTIVE AS A THERAPY FOR DIABETES."

"THE A-BOMB WAS DROPPED ON 'SHIMA AND—"

"AS A THERAPY —"

"—AND IT WENT THROUGH ALBERT CAMUS'S FUCKING CHEST!"

Silence. Paul, wild-eyed, is glaring at me. He lunges for me. I am startled and pull back but he is going to fall to the ground so I catch him. I am on the floor on both knees with him over me, his legs still on the bed. I am amazed at how light he feels. His hands go to my throat and he starts to strangle me. Or as best he can, which isn't much. He begins to sob in a most pathetic way.

"It's all right, Paul, I'm sorry," I whisper. "It's all right, it's all right. I'm sorry. In 1921 they didn't discover insulin. In 1921 Sacco and Vanzetti were sentenced to death. Sacco and Vanzetti, Paul, Sacco and Vanzetti, Sacco and Vanzetti."

He relaxes his grip but continues to sob. His heavy tears are dripping on my face. I lift and push him back onto his bed.

"Sacco and Vanzetti, Paul, Sacco and Vanzetti. It's all right. I'm sorry. Sacco and Vanzetti, Sacco and

Vanzetti, Sacco and Vanzetti, Sacco and Vanzetti."

He lets go of my throat. I wipe my face carefully with a Kleenex and then I take a wet facecloth and gently wipe his face and then I comb his hair with my fingers.

"It's all right, Paul. Sacco and Vanzetti, Sacco and Vanzetti, Sacco and Vanzetti, Sacco and Vanzetti, Sacco and Vanzetti."

I improvise a grim story. Sometimes our stories are short on plot, but through certain details left unexplained, through certain fertile ambiguities, they nonetheless resonate beautifully, like a painting, static but rich. Here it's not at all like that. There is little plot and little meaning. The story just stumbles along, unbelievable, unexplainable. Loretta Roccamatio drowns herself.

1921—Nicola Sacco and Bartolomeo Vanzetti, both poor Italian immigrants and anarchists, are found guilty and sentenced to death for two murders committed during a robbery in South Braintree, Massachusetts. In spite of flaws in the evidence, irregularities at their trial, accusations that the judge and jury are prejudiced against their political beliefs and social status, evidence that points to a group known as the Morelli gang, in spite of worldwide protests and appeals for clemency, Sacco and Vanzetti will be executed in 1927.

Paul is put on anti-depressants—amitriptyline at first,

then domipramine. It will take about two weeks before they become effective. In the meantime he is kept under close surveillance, especially at night, when he sleeps only in fits. Just in case, just in case. The clinical psychologist comes by nearly every afternoon. I call Paul about eight times a day.

1922—Benito Mussolini, whose Fascist squadristi have been provoking and intensifying an anarchic situation in Italy, receives a telegram from King Victor Emmanuel III. Il Duce is in power.

"Sometimes I can feel them in my blood. I can feel every virus as it courses through me, as it goes up my arms, across my chest, into my heart and then shoots out to my legs. And I can't do anything. I just lie here, waiting, waiting, knowing it's going to get worse."

He is fragile, so fragile. I give in to him again.

1923—Germany is incapable of making its payments on the war reparations imposed by the Allies in the Treaty of Versailles (set at 132 billion marks, roughly 33 billion dollars). France and Belgium occupy the Ruhr district to force compliance. The German government blocks all reparation deliveries and encourages passive resistance. The French and Belgians respond with mass arrests and an economic blockade that cuts off most of the occupied Rhineland from the rest of Germany. The German economy is devastated. By the end of 1923 a loaf of bread in Berlin costs 140 billion marks. The Weimar Republic is foundering. The ground is fertile for extremists.

Paul is waiting for me. He is bored. Strange how this illness, which aims to rob him of time, leaves him with so much of it on his hands.

1924—Lenin dies of sclerosis at the age of fifty-four. Stalin, whom Lenin had unsucessfully tried to have removed as Secretary General of the Communist Party, starts the edification of the Lenin myth, thus portraying himself as Lenin's great defender.

I bump into Paul's parents as I'm leaving the hospital. I have gotten to know the Atseas quite well. They have taken to me, as I have to them. I used to call ahead and ring at the door when I came to visit Paul at home, but quickly I was given a key and told that I was welcome any hour of the day or night, seven days a week, three hundred and sixty-five days a year. It's as though I have three parents now instead of one: Jack pats me on the back and Mary smiles at me and touches my forearm lightly. They inform me that there are sugarcane yogurts in the fridge now, my favourite, for when I come to their house next.

1925—Hitler publishes Mein Kampf.

I should have gone for a better story. Paul seems to be

improving. His Kaposi is uncertain, but his diarrhea is nearly gone.

1926—Rudolph Valentino, through the interces-sion of appendicitis, enters immortality at the age of thirty-one in New York City. Valentino came to the United States from Italy in 1913 and worked for a time as a gardener, as a dishwasher, as a dancer in vaudeville. In 1918 he went to Hollywood, where he played small parts in films until he was given the role of Julio in The Four Horsemen of the Apoca-lypse *(1921). He immediately became one of the greatest stars of the silent-movie era. His death causes hysteria, several suicides, and riots at his lying in state, which attracts an eleven-block-long crowd.*

Paul *is* feeling better. He has an appetite and hardly any diarrhea. And his Kaposi is looking fantastic. He shows me his left foot. The lighter lesions are gone and the big-ger ones are smaller and paler in colour. And, most important, he's in a great mood. On a Saturday morning I'm at the hospital with his family. They are animated and happy: Paul's coming home. He has just received a transfusion and he feels fine. He puts on his street clothes, which he hasn't worn in several weeks. They fit him loosely. His pants look like they're empty and his shirt dangles on his frame. I notice it, we all notice it, but we all ignore it. Paul walks a bit unsteadily; there are plenty of arms willing to support him. He smiles a lot and talks a lot.

> *1927—The near-bankrupt picture company of Warner Brothers releases* The Jazz Singer, *with Al Jolson. In an otherwise silent feature film, they add a recorded musical accompaniment, four singing sequences and a little dialogue that replaces the title cards and helps move the plot along. For the first time, sound is integrated with plot and narration becomes more fluid and gripping. The movie is an enormous success. The talking-pictures' era has begun.*

To do something, to pass the time, to assert control, Paul and I rearrange his room. He gives orders, I execute them. We make a circus of it. I huff and puff while lifting a book, then move the bed pretending it's nothing. Paul laughs, the aim of it all.

Nineteen twenty-eight is Paul's year and a very good year it is. Suffrage is extended to women in Great Britain; the Kellogg-Briand Pact, which outlaws aggressive war as an instrument of national policy, is signed in Paris by sixty-three countries; Amelia Earhart flies across the Atlantic, the first woman to do so; the Hungarian bio-chemist Albert von Szent-Gyorgyi discovers Vitamin C; Canada's Percy Williams is the sensation of the Amster-dam Olympics, winning gold medals in the 100-metre and 200-metre sprints; Ravel's *Bolero* is a universal hit—

yes, it could only be a good story for the Roccamatios.

1928—The world meets Mickey Mouse in the first animated sound cartoon, Steamboat Willie, *by Walt Disney and Ub Iwerks. Disney and Iwerks have actually already made two silent cartoons with a cheerful, energetic mouse—*Plane Crazy, *in which the mouse is called Mortimer Mouse, and* Galloping Gaucho—*but when they see* The Jazz Singer, *they recognize the limitless possibilities of sound in animated cartoons, put these two silent shorts aside and quickly produce* Steamboat. *It is a hit.*

Paul shows me some photos. The second one is of two boys, fifteenish, sitting in a pile of orange and brown leaves, dressed in jeans and heavy sweaters. They both have wide, slightly demented grins.

"That's James, my best friend in high school, on the left and that's me on the right."

I manage to check my gasp. But I stare. I try to find one point of resemblance—the hair, the chin, the nose, the glint of the eyes, anything—but there's nothing, nothing at all. Paul Photo and Paul Beside Me are two different people. Paul Beside Me doesn't notice my horror. Nothing evokes the past, rejuvenates the sick, raises the very dead, like a collection of family photographs. These flashbacks to a healthy past, to a time of energy, pleasure and clear skin, cheer up Paul. I stare at the other photos of this stranger without saying a word.

We go for walks, slow walks. Paul moves carefully, dragging his feet lightly, feeling the terrain to avoid any tiring jerks. Fortunately, the spring weather is dazzling. Paul is bowled over by the beauty of expanses of green grass. His optimism is radiant and fragile. I make 1929 a fun story.

1929—The Belgian Georges Remi, better known as Hergé, creates Tintin. It is a wonderful creation. In twenty-three albums, from Tintin au Pays des Soviets *in 1929 to* Tintin et les Picaros *in 1976, the rich, detailed, beautifully coloured Tintin cosmology unfolds—and enraptures. General de Gaulle will confess one day to André Malraux that Tintin* "est mon seul rival international."

Paul has been home for over two weeks. The house is like a solar system, with Paul's bedroom or, more precisely, Paul, as the sun, the centre of it all. In every important place in the house there is an interphone that is linked to his room. The system is on all the time. There is a quiet static in the air and every rustle, every cough, every word that the Sun King produces is heard throughout his domain. The kitchen is littered with his culinary whims, quantities of wasted delicious food. Medical journals— he has subscriptions to *Nature, Scientific American, The New England Journal of Medicine, The Lancet* and more; he even gets papers from the Pasteur Institute—which his parents secretly loathe but which he reads assiduously, are in bookshelves, on tables, on the floor. His things—a sweater, a half-drunk glass of orange juice, an open book, slippers, an unfinished crossword puzzle, a portable electronic game—are everywhere, left not because he is spoiled but because he is tired and forgetful. The routine of the household, as regards his parents and Jennifer, is medico-military: everything is on time, structured, well done. The aides-de-camp relay themselves in gently waking their commander-in-chief at precisely midnight so that he can take his AZT. This isn't a sharing of a burden: it's that they all want their turn.

Paul talks of starting his studies again. By correspondence or, better, part-time at York University. We're enthusiastic. He wants to major in philosophy and film.

1930—The American Clyde Tombaugh discovers the ninth planet of our solar system, Pluto.

The Roccamatios are interrupted for eight days. Paul and his parents have left for their Georgian Bay cottage.

"It's for my white cells," he tells me. "They don't want to go up. Big spaces, fresh air—it'll be good for them."

His optimism seems tired.

1931 is my year but Paul asks to do it. My story is trite and strikes me as inappropriate—the American J. Schick invents the electric razor—and I feel sad that day so I let him have it. Just before he leaves, he tells me a brief, puzzling story, and afterwards, when he is gone, I feel even sadder.

1931—Kurt Gödel publishes Über Formal unentscheidbare Sätze der Principia Mathematica und verwandter Systeme, *showing that in any formal mathematical system in which elementary arithmetic can be done, there are propositions whose truth or falsity cannot be proved on the basis of the axioms within that system, and therefore that the basic axioms of arithmetic may give rise to contradictions.*

Jack and Mary rush Paul back to Toronto. He has abdominal pains that keep him bent in two. They drive him directly to the hospital.

A count of five hundred white cells. Christ. Next to no immunity protection left. He's wide open. He receives a transfusion.

1932—Paul Doumer, President of France, is shot twice by a Russian immigrant, Pavel Gorgulov, and dies of his injuries.

It's a ridiculous thing to put in a balance, but in the balance of things I suppose it's better to be losing a brother than a son. A child dying before a parent, the future before the past—can there be anything more debilitating? It is worse than death, it is the ultimate hopelessness: it is extinction. No one adapts well to morbidity, but Jennifer is doing it the least badly. As it has with me, Paul's illness has throttled her whistling, youthful insouciance. She is more deliberate, her spontaneity is fitful and highstrung.

She tells me that often at night she worries about the small, fatal risks of ordinary life and can't fall asleep for them. They terrify her not for her own sake—as you might think—but for her parents'. With Paul going, she feels a silent pressure from Jack and Mary: love. She feels that she mustn't at any cost let them down and die. She doesn't ride her bicycle any more for fear of sewer grates and swinging car doors.

I don't want to deal with 1933. It's easy to relax so why don't we relax? I bring an oriental game that a friend has recently taught me called Go. The rules are very simple—you play with black and white beads on a criss-cross board; the aim is to surround your enemy—but the game is as complex as chess, only more accessible to beginners. I think Paul might get into it. But he just interrupts me.

"You've forgotten something, haven't you?"

"I don't feel like it."

"Oh no you don't. It's 1933. Do you know what happened in 1933?"

"You mean the beginning of the New Deal legislation?"

"Try again."

"Edwin Armstrong invents FM radio?"

"One more time."

"The rumba is the craze?"

"Again."

"Welcome King Kong and false eyelashes?"

Paul kidnaps my year. Marco achieves majority control over Orlando's group of small shareholders and forces Orlando off the board of directors.

1933—Hitler becomes chancellor. The Third Reich is proclaimed from Potsdam. The first concentration camp is opened on the site of a former ammunitions factory in Dachau. Between 1933 and 1945 it will hold more than 206,000 registered prisoners. Besides the thousands killed before registration or sent for extermination elsewhere, 32,000 men, women and children will die at Dachau.

Since Paul took 1933, I take 1934, his year, and keep 1935. I impose myself. There is no greater, more beautiful surprise than the strength of love one discovers one has for a newborn baby. I announce the birth of Lars Roccamatio!

1934—In a poor French-Canadian farmhouse near Callander, Ontario, the Dionne Quintuplets— Annette, Cecile, Emilie, Yvonne and Marie—are born. And live. No sets of identical quints in the history of the world (all two of them) have ever survived for more than a few hours. The news amazes and delights a world in need of good news. Gifts of money, clothes, food, breast milk, equipment and advice begin to pour in from all sides. The Red Cross builds a special, ultramodern hospital for them across from their farmhouse. But people want to see, see for themselves, these miraculous mites. The world begins to move in on the Dionnes. They become the biggest tourist attraction in Canada, bigger than Niagara Falls. The Ontario government of Mitch Hepburn, concerned with protecting the children from exploitation (or is it "concerned with protecting the exploitation of the children"?), passes the Dionne Quintuplet Act, which makes them wards of the province, and appoints a board of guardians. The hospital is expanded and becomes the centre of a complex called "Quintland". Tourists come and come and come, as many as 6,000 a day, 3 million in all, to see the cutesome five through one-way glass as they gambol about their special playground. The tourists spend 51 million dollars in 1934, double that two years later, a total estimated in 1944 at half a billion dollars. Real-estate values soar in Callander. Hotels, motels, restaurants and souvenir shops proliferate. Those who can't make the trip to see the Quints live can see them in their three Hollywood movies or in the Fox-Movietone newsreels or on the covers of countless magazines or in the advertisements of the various products they endorse: canned milk, syrup, dolls, baby clothes, soap, breakfast foods, baby foods, etc. From India to Germany to Ethiopia, Callander becomes the best-known—if not the only known—Canadian city. Forget Hitler and Mussolini, the world wants to know how their sweet Quints are today. Yes, there will be troubles later on, the price of too many people, too much money, too little love—but still, the Dionne Quints are the nicest thing to happen to Canada during the thirties.

Then I go for the excitement of a high-powered crisis at Helsinki City Hall.

1935—Conservative Prime Minister R.B. Bennett calls a federal election. Since Confederation his administration has come the closest to being a one-man, quasi-dictatorial show. A millionaire many times over, he used his own resources to get his party elected in the 1930 election. He also flatly guaranteed that he would solve the problems of the Depression. "I'll use tariffs to blast a way into the markets that have been closed to you," "I'll blast a way through all our difficulties," he said. In 1935 people who can no longer afford gasoline remove the engines from their cars and hitch the cars to horses; they're called "Bennett buggies". In 1935 the Canadian people blast away Bennett. The Conservatives go down to their worst defeat ever: 40 seats, a loss of 97 in a House of 245 seats. William Lyon Mackenzie King is Prime Minister again.

Paul is hardly listening to me. I hear a swallowing. I look up from the little notes I have prepared for my story and I see his eyes are red and his lips are trembling. I stop.

"Ohhhh," he whispers with difficulty, "I just want to live. I'll give up my ambitions." He starts to cry. "I don't c-care if I make nothing of my life, I'll do any l-l-l-lousy job, anything."

I have seen it before, it has happened before, often, but for some reason, at that moment, I am not prepared for it. I panic. I get up, I move towards the door (to get someone?), I sit down again, I get up, I sit on the bed.

"I just want t-time."

I want to speak but the words (what words?) are stuck in my throat, I want to cry too, but I feel that I mustn't so I don't, I stand up, I take hold of the glass of water on his bedside table.

"I w-wish I had a g-g-girlfriend."

I sit down, I put the glass back on the table, I put my hand on his hand, I get up, I sit down.

"I can't take it any more, I just can't take it any more."

I stand up, I look at the curtains of the room (maybe I should close them?), I sit down.

"Paul!"—I can finally manage some words—"Paul, you have to hang on till they find a cure. You just have to hang on. You know how many hundreds of millions of dollars are going into research all over the world. I mean in the U.S., in France, in Germany, in Holland, here in Canada, everywhere. Scientists are on to this thing like never before for anything else. It's like a huge Manhattan Project. The biggest brains around. They're making new discoveries *every* day. You know that. Time is on your side, Paul. Hang in there!"

He starts to calm down. We talk for a long time. He falls asleep. I change my story.

1935—The Depression is still on, hard.

I look out the window of the bus as I am heading home. I can't believe I said that. "Time is on your side." Fuck.

1936—The Spanish Civil War begins.

Jack never manages the trick, if trick there is. He is a member of that square, hard-working war generation that commands hefty salaries nowadays and thanks to whose wealth-producing toil my generation has had it good and easy. Jack is a kind, intelligent man whose happiness operated within a structure. When a bomb shattered that structure to small pieces, he and his happiness fell apart. He is the one who has adapted the least well to Paul's illness. Quite simply, he can't accommodate the pain. It destabilizes him continually. He struggles, and I mean struggles, to cope. He is a fragile man, with a hollow look in his eyes and his hair whiter than before. And he is on anti-depressants, just like his son.

1937—Japan invades China.

Paul has received yet another transfusion. He experiences a moment of strength and—directly related—of euphoria. For 1938 I am expecting a Kristallnacht story but he surprises me.

"You'll like my story," he tells me. And I do.

1938—Ladislao and George Biro patent the ball-point pen.

Tests, tests, tests. Bad result: lack of oxygen in the blood. Possibly a relapse of PCP. We don't say anything. He is scared. So am I. His breathing is quick and shallow. So is mine.

1939—Professor Antanas Smetona, the president of independent Lithuania, broadcasts a last speech over the radio, protesting his country's annexation by the Soviet Union, which will be a brutal affair—one quarter of the gulag will be composed of Lithuanians by the end of the 1940s. Smetona does not want to make his speech in Lithuanian, which no one outside his small country will understand. But he also refuses to speak the tongues of the oppressors, Russian, Polish or German. Smetona makes his last speech in Latin.

I walk around the hospital. To prepare myself. Something will come up. It won't happen, it won't end that way. I breathe deeply. Amazing remissions have been reported. In some desperate cases of cancer, for example. Why not here? I see people lying in beds. Many of them watch me as I walk by, their heads turned, their eyes wide open. Why are they here? Do they have *it*? I don't want to know. I go down a staircase, am approaching Paul's area. There *are* medical miracles. At the end of a corridor I see an old man sitting on a chair beneath a window. He is waiting. He is gently rocking himself from side to side. He looks about meekly. He is holding a small, brown paper bag. Some pastry, some treat or other, I imagine. I smile at him. He is not very well dressed. He waits with infinite patience. Where's your son or daughter, old man? Being examined? Scanner perhaps? Was it sex? Sharing needles? Looking at the man, I am overwhelmed by the feeling that he is of no importance. A loser. He could die, his son or daughter could die, and it wouldn't matter in the least to anyone. Behold the suffering of the man of no importance. Behold the solitude of pain. I feel a sinking in me. I can't face Paul yet. I walk some more.

1940 — Doctor Karl Brandt receives a single-paragraph letter from high up. "(N)amentlich zu bestimmende Ärzte" *(Doctors to be designated) are to be authorized so that* "unheilbar Kranken bei kritischster Beurteilung ihres Krankheitszustandes der Gnadentod gewährt werden kann" *(mercy killing can be administered to patients who are terminally ill, as far as can be determined after a thorough and rigorous examination of their state of health). Operation T4—*(Paul interrupts himself. "Isn't that an extraordinary coincidence?" he says. "T4. Exactly like the cells in the immune system that are attacked by the HIV. Isn't that extraordinary! I say, I say.")—*operation T4 is set in motion. A home for the physically handicapped run by the Samaritans is taken over and transformed. Early in the year, Graffeneck opens, the first of six euthanasia centres (Hadamar, Brandenburg, Hartheim, Sonnenstein, Bernburg). At Graffeneck, 9,839 "terminally ill" patients will die—mostly mentally retarded men, women and children. At least 60,000 will die in the whole operation. This euthanasia pogrom will end, officially, in August of the next year after protests from church groups. But almost immediately the technology, experience and personnel will be transferred outside the country. To Poland, for example.*

1941—Marshall Pétain institutes Mother's Day.

Mary has developed a limited resilience. She has faith in hope. When her hope is troubled, when the unthinkable forces itself upon her, she seems to find some inner something and—diminished, permanently saddened—still manage to go on. Certainly more than Jack anyway. Maybe she is religious, I don't know. I am careful never to talk about religion. Who am I to kick at people's crutches?

Paul has stopped shaving. He has been losing his hair and it hasn't been growing back. The doctors offer, want, to shave him bald—"We always recommend it. It will depress him less than going bald hair by hair"—but he bursts into tears and refuses.

1942—Blacks are accepted for the first time in the

American army: the American army enters the Second World War.

A lumbar puncture isn't supposed to hurt—it didn't the last time—but Paul screams. They have to go at it twice before they can get the needle in right. I think I'm cool—I look Jack and Mary in the eyes and tell them it doesn't really hurt, he's just being oversensitive, and it's for a good purpose, it'll help in establishing a diagnostic, and it's harmless and it doesn't take long and everything will be all right—I think I'm cool, but when I go to drink I can't hold any water in my paper cup, my hand is trembling so much. Finally I bend over and drink from the tap. It turns out Paul has a fungus called *Cryptococcus neoformans* in his spinal fluid. There is a risk of meningo-encephalitis. The thing could go to his head. They are going to keep a close watch. At the smallest sign he will be put on amphotericin B and flucytosine.

I start my story—Monika Roccamatio is on a train, alone in her compartment, when a dignified, disfigured man, with a face like a skull and a right hand that is gloved in spite of the warm weather, steps in and sits down; and eventually they begin a conversation—I start my story, but for the first time I can't complete it. Every time I am about to speak I feel a heat in my eyes and a tightness in my throat. I abandon the story—Monika simply vanishes from the family—but I'm lucky—Paul is exhausted and drops to sleep. He is very pale.

1943—The Final Solution.

My good health, what an insolence.

1944—Antoine de Saint-Exupéry, author of Le
Petit Prince, *disappears with his plane somewhere
between Corsica and Savoy while on a reconnais-
sance mission.*

The side effects are too serious: Paul stops taking AZT.
He is happy about it since he feels better. The announcement stuns me. There is not even the fiction of a cure
now. I sit beside his bed trying to contain myself. I do
not, but do not, want to talk about it. I am so afraid he is
going to interrupt me, I have difficulty getting my story
out. I can hear my voice trembling. It is the shortest of all
the Roccamatio stories, a murder. Paul is pleased.

1945—Hiroshima.

After the hospital, I tramp about the streets of Toronto,
salivating with nihilism. I catch the headlines at a news-
stand—blood in Sri Lanka, the West Bank, Haiti, Iran,
Iraq; the Ku Klux Klan wins an election in Louisiana;
bored youths riot in Switzerland; there's a picture of a
Japanese lumber-processing ship on the Amazon
River—and I am delighted. It starts me off. The world is
metastasizing! We are not a viable species! I exult at the
shrinking of tropical rain forests and the expansion of the

Sahara and the emptying of the seas. Long live the green-
house effect and acid rain and crack and pollution and
religion. Hail Mister Escobar! Hail Mister Wojtyla! Boo
the white rhinoceros and boo Amnesty International. In
Pol Pot and Shining Path we trust. THREE CHEERS FOR
APATHY! And what's wrong with apartheid, I mean the
South African apartheid? It's just another credit card, no
worse than American Express. And Mister Gorbachev,
when would you like the West Edmonton Mall? You'll
find that it solves most human problems. As for the
depletion of nonrenewable natural resources—I love it,
can't get enough of it. Petroleum, natural gas, coal, liter-
acy, peat moss, fish, ozone, minerals, arable land, ura-
nium, timber, oxygen—to hell with them! Me and my
ten billion brothers and sisters will wing it on Hail
Marys, Cheez Whiz and television. And if we fail, well
then, thank God for the exit of death. Yes, thank God for
death. Welcome death, oh welcome. Shine on me!

This attack starts to wear off. Where am I? I am on
Bloor, not far from Brunswick. A shaft of sunlight breaks
through the clouds of this warm, summer afternoon and
irradiates the façade of some Lebanese greasy spoon. I am
surprised. I feel something in me unwinding. Nearly
against my will, I like what I'm looking at. I look at the
slightly rundown but clean place, at the window where a
few ads—yoga lessons, rock bands, used books—are
taped, where grease spots and grit are made visible by the
sunlight. Inside, a slim Middle-Eastern-type man with a
beautifully thick moustache is preparing a falafel in pita

for a red-haired young woman dressed in black with black-rimmed glasses. I like this banal, wonderful scene, want a falafel in pita, want to chat up the young woman. A bum with a twenty-foot-radius sphere of stink assaults my nose and asks me for some spare change. I smile, say, "Sure," and give him a dollar, telling him not to spend it on drink, to which he replies, "Sure," and staggers off. Yes, I smile. Then I walk up the street, looking at the people and at the stores. I'm dazzled by the multifarious variety of the human thing. There's a smell of curry. A perfume wafts by. I stop and I enjoy the smell of my sweat, the solidity of my body, the flexibility of my fingers and arms, I have a slight erection, I feel like masturbating, I crack my toes, I stretch, I lick my lips—I stop and I exult in the stupid, brute fact of my existence.

But don't get me wrong: it's that I've developed a capacity to enjoy catastrophe.

1946—War is declared in Indochina.

"Look at this," says Paul. His skeletal hand slowly reaches for the top of his head. His fingers assemble a strand of hair. He pulls. There is a little resistance, then the strand comes out cleanly. "It makes the funniest little sound. You can't hear it, but it makes the funniest little sound inside my head."

1947—As a prelude to the termination of British rule, India is partitioned to accommodate the fears and aspirations of the subcontinent's Hindus and Muslims. And so India achieves independence and Pakistan (Land of the Pure) is created. But Pakistan is geographically absurd: East Pakistan (formerly East Bengal, now Bangladesh) is more than a thousand miles from West Pakistan. Worse still, the delineation of the new borders through the intermeshed and irreconcilable communities of Bengal and Punjab envenoms an already violent conflict between Hindus and Muslims. There is a massive flow of refugees—seven to eight million Muslims leave India for Pakistan; about the same number of Hindus make the journey in reverse—and terrible acts of violence take place. Over two hundred thousand people are killed.

Paul's horizons are shrinking. There can be no question any more of foreign travel. Going home is travel. Leaving his hospital room is travel. He hardly has the strength to walk. Only to the bathroom to relieve himself; and even that.... The space beside his bed is becoming a horizon.

1948—Gandhi is assassinated.

Jack has always been a local history buff, but since Paul's illness it has become his passion. The Family Compact, the real Laura Secord, the inflexible Sir Francis Bond Head, the great Sir Isaac Brock ("Did you know he came from the Channel Islands?")—with these and more Jack is endlessly fascinated, and he shares this fascination with me and I encourage him and listen attentively and ask thoughtful questions, although nothing interests me less than the Family Compact, the real Laura Secord, the inflexible Sir Francis Bond Head or the great Sir Isaac Brock ("Jersey?" "No, Guernsey.") I love the man because of his pain. When we talk about the Battle of Queenston Heights or the tragic Tecumseh or the eccentric Thomas Talbot, I come away with the impression that we have been talking about Paul.

1949—Josef Stalin turns seventy, the occasion for worldwide Communist celebrations. The Stalin Peace Prizes are set up.

Get away, pain.

1950—Under the indifferent eyes of the world, China invades Tibet.

Paul is afflicted with hiccups. These involuntary spasmodic jerks drain him completely. He has neither the strength to stay awake nor the peace to fall asleep. He floats in some horrible limbo. The doctors try drugs. Then hypnosis. They are very worried.

The Roccamatios are interrupted for two weeks.

When things are at their worst, they suddenly get better. Paul seems to have entered a period of exhausted stability. Like a miracle, his hiccuping has stopped. And his diarrhea too, nearly; I suppose he has no more liquids to lose. His lungs—always a worry; one man in the hospital has had seven bouts of PCP—are all right. He's been off alpha interferon since long ago and his Kaposi has spread, but the nearest mirror is far, far away and, anyway, he's too tired to care—it's the least painful of his problems. He is under perfusion—vitamins, minerals, etc.—sleeps a lot and rarely gets out of bed. Like a pregnant woman, he has sudden whims for particular foods, but he can hardly hold them down, vomits often.

1950 is the last year that Paul takes full responsibility for a Roccamatio story. He can simply no longer sustain the effort of concentration. He stops reading, he stops creating. He becomes the critical, obtrusive spectator of my imagination. My only respite is that he tires easily, unbelievably easily. He falls asleep at any moment, even in mid-sentence. He doesn't particularly want to sleep; it's more that it's the favourite state of his exhausted body. Sometimes I wait ten minutes or so—time for him to rest a little and forget what he has been saying—and then I wake him and continue my story; other times—and more frequently as the years go by—I whisper my story knowing he is sleeping.

1951—The Arab League's political committee appeals to its member states to tighten their economic blockade of Israel and, especially, to shut off oil supplies.

Paul finds urinating painful. They check his catheter. Nothing wrong. Some urinary tract infection. Even that simple pleasure will be denied him.

> *1952—The Supreme Court of South Africa invalidates the race legislation of Doctor (in divinity) Daniel F. Malan, Prime Minister since 1948. This legislation institutionalizes the system of "apartness" that has been governing in practice the relations between the races since well before the creation of the Union of South Africa in 1910. Shortly after the court's move, Parliament approves a government-sponsored bill to restrict the powers of the Supreme Court. Malan, and his successor, Johannes Strijdom, will thereafter pursue the construction of apartheid, but it will be perfectly finished by Professor (of applied psychology and sociology; the brilliant scholar) Hendrik Verwoerd, Prime Minister from 1958 to 1966.*

Paul doesn't eat any more. Sometimes he sucks on an ice-cube. I arrive eating a chocolate bar, a Mars, not thinking about it. Paul stares at me, at my fingers, at my mouth. He doesn't seem to understand, as if eating has become an incomprehensible activity to him. I don't know what to do. I know that if he takes any, he will vomit. But the look in his eyes! Finally, I take the smallest flake of chocolate, a mere ripple off the top, and I carefully place it on the tip of his tongue. I do this with trepidation, as if Paul were a bomb and I were about to trip him. The flake sticks to Paul's pasty tongue. He pulls, he *pulls* his tongue in—I can sense the effort in everything that he does. A few seconds go by. The flake is melting; saliva is wetting Paul's mouth. Suddenly he breathes out and opens his mouth and closes his eyes. Nausea! I quickly run my finger over his tongue and remove the half-melted flake. I put another finger in the glass beside his bed and wet Paul's tongue with a few drops of lemon-flavoured water. He remains with his eyes closed. He is on an edge, an edge between nausea and pain on one side and tired numbness on the other. I wait. He opens his eyes. He is in no pain. I smile. "It's bad for you anyway. Cavities." "Pimples too," he replies. He manages a smile. He's in a good mood! At the National High School Debating Competition, held in Turku, Georgio Roccamatio triumphs in the debate "Is television an anti-democratic medium?" and receives the President Kekkonen Award from President Koivisto himself, who tells him he is expecting a call from him the day he turns eighteen.

1953—Dag Hammarskjöld is elected Secretary General of the United Nations.

The transfusion is slow, takes time, but Paul's system takes the shock. He feels stronger, better.

Paul vomits, vomits blood.

"Internal hemorrhage," drops the nurse.

I can't close my eyes. I can feel them like huge spheres

staring out. I can't close them or turn them. There is blood and liquid on the bedsheet, on Paul's hand. The nurse puts on plastic gloves. They're a horrible transparent white. Suddenly I'm afraid—of Paul's blood, of Paul himself. I get to my feet, mutter that I will be back and leave the room. I head for the bathroom. I lock myself in. I start to roll up my sleeves but then I simply take my shirt off. Someone knocks. I turn my head and look at the door, bewildered. "It's busy. There's no one here," I hush inaudibly. With hot water and plenty of soap I begin to wash meticulously my hands, my arms, my face. I bring my hands right up to my face and inspect every square millimetre, searching for the least cut, nick, abrasion or blemish.

"There's this"—pause—"burning inside me," he whispers when I get back.

When I make to leave, I place my hand on Paul's sheet over his chest and very gently tap, as if in sympathy for this burning inside him. In fact, I don't want to touch his hand. Then, at home, for the hundredth time, for the thousandth time, I read that there is no empirical evidence, none, none at all, that it can be passed on through casual contact. I sit down and I consciously go about quelling my panic.

1954—The first hydrogen bomb is exploded by the Americans, in the Marshall Islands.

I have thought about it. Not in bed, that's for sure.

Better a bang than a whimper. Better to be shot in the street in broad daylight by my enemies. Suddenly, just like that, as I'm turning a streetcorner, seven bullets in the chest.

1955—James Dean dies in a car crash.

Suddenly, just like that, Paul is in pain. It comes from nowhere. One moment he's fine and the next he's in pain. I feel like shouting and waving my arms and putting on an ugly expression, as if the pain were a mugger I could frighten away. But I can do nothing, except wait and watch.

"It h … hurts," he moans (what? where?), fixing me with his eyes. He stares at me as if he would hold on to me. If I should break eye contact I think Paul would fall, would fall into death. I don't break eye contact.

1956—The U.S.S.R. invades Hungary.

Paul is resting. At any rate, his eyes are closed. There is silence except for the slight rasp of his breathing, and my swallowing, which only I can hear. I am sitting, my arms crossed, my legs crossed, motionless. I want to scream.

His eyes open, directly looking at me. I smile wanly.

"Hi," I say, faintly.

He has chosen this day to talk about God.

"Do you believe in God?" he whispers.

I uncross myself and lean forward. I take note of his

tone of voice. I am a perfect turncoat and I lie with perfect conviction.

"Yes. I do."

There is a pause.

"I think me too," comes a clipped response. He seems relieved. Tiny little beads of sweat cover his forehead. Every time he swallows, he closes his eyes. He has forgotten all our apostatic arguments at university.

"I believe God is everywhere. In every manifestation of life," I add, seamlessly.

"Me too."

"God flows through time. There is neither Before nor After. Spirit is timeless."

"Yes."

"He cares for us all."

He swallows and falls asleep.

1957—After enduring six years of smears and baseless attacks, the Canadian diplomat Herbert Norman commits suicide by jumping off the roof of an apartment building in Cairo. McCarthyism adds another Canadian to its list of victims.

I drop by the office of the hospital chaplain. There is a nice, bland woman at the desk. I inform her that Patient Paul, Room So-and-so, Wing So-and-so, would probably appreciate the mock-fortuitous, easygoing visit of Charlie Chaplain. "Easy does it, baby," I feel like adding. "We don't want him reading *The Watchtower*, eh?" But I just shut up. I only ask what his visiting hours are. To make damn sure that I never bump into him.

"Why don't I eat any more?" Paul asks me. "They should give me a drug that makes me hungry. It must exist. They should feed me, don't you think?"

Before I can answer, he falls asleep. Beside his bed is the latest meal he hasn't touched.

1958—Pasternak "voluntarily" declines his Nobel Prize. And is abused and harassed by the Soviet government until his death two years later.

This disease that leaves you no respite, that eats, eats, eats away, that attacks your breathing and digestion and spinal cord and sullies your skin, that attacks you everywhere—but slowly, slowly, nothing quick, no sudden push into eternity—this slow, inhumane attrition—he's at the bottom of his bed, he can't walk any more, he can't control his pissing or shitting, he labours to breathe, he weighs seventy-one pounds and dropping, his skin is a horror of coloured scabs and lesions, you don't want to touch him any more, when you look at him you think of garbage spilt on the street—overripe fruit, moulding cheese, putrid meat—yet from amidst this putrefaction a quavering voice weakly clamours its humanity by calling out your name—this disease—you can't *imagine* the degradation—this disease, it's enough, in the absence of anything holier, to make me want to piss on a crucifix.

"What's to be done? Another transfusion? He isn't strong enough. A perfusion to feed him? Fine. We're doing that. But he can't even tolerate the least medicine any more." So say the doctors.

Paul's arms are covered in Band-aids, blue spots, black scabs, the legacies of tests, tranfusions, perfusions. His skin is like a livid, translucent rainbow. Every shade of black, brown, purple, blue, green, yellow. The rings around his eyes are enormous concentric circles. "Tell me, doctor," I feel like asking, "how does skin get *green*?"

1959—Swiss male voters defeat a constitutional amendment to allow women to vote in national elections.

I was hoping to start the new decade with a brighter story, but Paul is having troubles with his eyes. Cytomegalovirus. Nothing to be done. He is overwhelmed by fear. He asks a nurse to strangle him. He is given nitrazepam; it is supposed to help against "acute anxiety".

"I wanna get out of here, I hate it, I'm sick of being their guinea-pig, I wanna get out, I wanna get out, I wanna get out, I wanna get out, I wanna get out, I wanna get out, I wanna get out, I wanna get out, I wanna get out, I wanna get out—"

He repeats it twenty, thirty, forty times.

I am stopping the Roccamatios. I want out.

I am so stressed I think I'm going to explode. "You

mean the boy has fever, diarrhea, pneumonia, Kaposi's sarcoma, cytomegalovirus, cryptococci, looks like a carnival-coloured skeleton, is as bald as a cue ball, has lost half his weight, is going blind AND YOU CAN'T DO SHIT!" I am having this imaginary conversation in my head with the doctors. "What the hell is all your science for? Do you know how much money we give you?" I leave the hospital trembling. "You're FRAUDS!" Outside I am walking on a gravel path. The crunching sound it makes annoys me so much I start pounding it with my feet and screaming at it. My legs begin to hurt. I run alongside a red brick wall. I stop. My back is to it. My hands and fingers feel like hooks. I feel like doing something with them, tearing something, destroying something. I wave them in front of my face. I am aware of the sound of my shirt cuffs flapping against my wrists. My mouth is wide open, as if for a scream but with no scream. I am shaking my head like an ape. I drop to my knees and I scratch the ground, driving the hard black earth under my fingernails. I am trembling, I am in a fetal position, I can feel the grit of the soil against my forehead and hairline. I calm down. I am still. "Oh doctors, please do your best."

I head home, crossing the suburbs of Toronto, of southern Ontario, those nightmare suburbs of comfort. In Paul's presence, close to death, I feel close to the jugular vein of life. So while I feel relieved when I leave him—it's like an escape from claustrophobia; a vital stretching; a dazed relaxing—I also feel depressed: I'm getting away from the edge of life, from the edge that *makes* life. Instead, I penetrate an environment that is cluttered with objects, cluttered with hollow niceness, a stifling environment that fills me, like a nausea, with only one powerful feeling: a twenty-first-century boredom. I head home, crossing the suburbs of Toronto, of southern Ontario. I think only of Paul and of the Roccamatios. I disrespect everything else.

There is a sign posted beside the door to Paul's room. "Mr. Atsea's visitors are informed that Mr. Atsea has gone blind. Could they please identify themselves as they enter." I can't believe my eyes. I head for the bathroom and stay there twenty minutes.

When I go in, Paul is lying there, waiting for me. His eyes are open. They turn my way. I am terribly nervous. I can't get any words out. Finally I can and I can't help myself.

"F... f... f... fuck, Paul, you're going blind."

And for the first time ever, I cry right in front of him. Great, cracking, uncontrollable sobs.

Who am I to need comfort, but he comforts me.

"Shhh, shhhh, it's all"—pause—"right." I can hardly hear him. "Whose turn"—pause—"is it? What year are we?" Pause. "Is it my turn?"

Oh, fuck everything. On the spur of the moment I make up a despairing story.

1961—Dag Hammarskjöld is killed in an airplane crash over the Congo while on a U.N. mission.

"Yes," is all Paul says. He has been receiving morphine shots every twelve hours.

Paul is in a wheelchair. It's his birthday today. He's going home, getting out of here. Bundled up in sweater, scarf, gloves, blanket, tuque and black sunglasses, all I can see of him is his nose and upper lip. It's mid-September and the weather is very pleasant. I'm not even wearing a jacket. With every jerk of the wheelchair he bounces like bones in a bag of skin.

Last thing I remember from the hospital: I am walking down the corridor for the last time. In one room I glimpse a trinket on a bedside table. A shiny pink porcelain hand holding a bright red heart. Why is so much about death in bad taste?

Paul is lucid. He is lying sideways on his bed at home. He is happy there, never wants to go back to the hospital. The room next door has been fixed up for the nurse who is there twenty-four hours a day.

"I'll do"—pause—"one more story," he whispers.

"We're at 1962."

"No." Pause. "You do that, I'll do"—pause—"another year."

"Which one? Do you want me to help you with the research?"

"No." Pause. "I'll do the year"—pause—"2001." Pause. "That'll make it"—pause—"a hundred years"—pause—"of Roccamatios."

"Great idea, Paul."

"Yes." Pause. "Who's left?"

By which I gather that he means which of the Roccamatios are left.

"Ingrid."

"The grand"—pause—"mother?"

"Yes. And Susanna, her grandniece, the actress."

"Oh."

"And Lars, her five-year-old son."

But Paul has fallen asleep, or unconscious, I don't know which, and he doesn't hear about Lars. He slips in and out now.

1962—Marilyn Monroe commits suicide.

I enter his room to the strain of "With a Little Help from My Friends". Beatle Paul is curled up on his side. Beatle George, faithful to the last, is lying on the floor beside him.

"The year 2001?" I ask.

"Not yet."

What can I say? He falls asleep to "Lucy in the Sky with Diamonds".

I put a pad of paper and a pen beside his hand on the bed.

Today it's "A Day in the Life". But he's asleep.

Death has a smell. It permeates the house.

"Paul?"

"I'm still"—pause—"thinking."

Jack has bought me a Ralph Lauren suit complete with shirts, ties, socks and shoes. He thinks I always dress like a beggar. His attitudes have changed a lot since the beginning of Paul's illness—he has taken leave from his job; he mocks his more staid colleagues; he's working on a lengthy essay called "The Dynamics of the Battles of the War of 1812"—but he's still not exactly artsy-fartsy granola bar. A few days ago I bought him a casual gift, Mishima's *Sea of Fertility* novels, secondhand, and he has jumped at the opportunity of returning my kindness. He puts his arm around my shoulders and finds comfort in giving me some father-son advice. Mercifully, he doesn't ask me what I intend to do with my future. I ask him a question about Egerton Ryerson.

"Paul?"

"Not"—pause—"yet."

I walk George H. I like walking dogs. It gives purpose to aimlessness. I can't stand it when people treat animals like human beings, yet irresistibly I find myself conversing with this creature, brain the size of a lemon. He doesn't seem as bouncy as usual. His tail is low and there is no enthusiasm to his sniffing. I think he may be losing weight. I take a stick, wave it in front of his face and throw it. He bounds after it and like any self-respecting ill-mannered dog he proceeds to chew the stick to pieces. He comes back with flakes of slobbered black bark hanging from his mouth. When we have returned home, I ask Mary if she doesn't think he's losing weight. We are in the kitchen, she has her back to me. She doesn't say anything. Then she turns around and glares at George H., who knows something's coming. She walks to a chair, sits down, grabs him by the ears and brings his head up to hers. She presses her dry, white nose against his wet, black one and stares into his bright, dumb eyes. "One sick person in this house is enough, George H." She points to his dish, which is brimming with canine-succulent food. "EAT!" she screams. And, half-heartedly it seems, George H. eats. I smile. I go down to the basement and cry.

"Please, Paul."

"I've"—pause—"got it." Pause. "But later." Sleep.

"Being for the Benefit of Mr. Kite." I just sit there, listening intently. The album starts over. Pulse: 160. Blood pressure: 60 over 30. He is dying. He is sleeping.

George H. has taken to lying on the bed, right near him but carefully out of his way. He whines quietly. I notice Paul's lips and nostrils are slightly blue. I ask the nurse about it.

"Cyanosis. Which means a lack of oxygen in the blood."

"Which means PCP."

She looks at me. And nods.

Oh man. All this to end with the beginning. A cycle for nothing, for nothing except protracted agony.

I find something scribbled on the pad but I can't make anything of it.

He is too weak to move or speak. He just lies there, his eyes blinking once in a while. He has had his morphine three hours before.

"Paul?"

I kneel right beside him.

"Paul, it's me."

His eyes blink and his mouth trembles.

I don't know what to say. Since my eyes are level with it, I gently start to play with his ear. I rub the lobe between my thumb and forefinger. Then, I gently run my finger inside his ear. The tip of my finger is shiny.

"I'll be back in a second."

I come back with several Q-tips. I gently clean Paul's ear, first the outside, then inside where the wax is yellow and deep brown. Paul's mouth trembles into an approximation of a smile.

"Don't worry, Paul," I whisper. "Soon, soon."

His lips move to make a word. There is no breath to create it. He struggles.

"Two." It barely comes out.

Two. For 2001.

It will be in a few days, hours. Not long at any rate.

For eight days I visit every day. Sometimes he comes to—once Mary even found him sitting up—and he manages to speak, but never when I am there. I ask in vague terms if he has said anything that was meant for me, but there's nothing.

Shortly before three in the morning George H. shatters the silence with a barking that is furious and incessant. Mary, who has fallen asleep on the sofa beside the bed, awakes instantly. The nurse, who checked on him an hour before, and Jack and Jennifer are in the room not five seconds later. George H. is straddling Paul, his tail erect, every hair on his back standing up, his teeth bared and his mouth salivating, looking, for the first time ever, menacing. It would have been the sixty-third story for the Roccamatios. The year JFK was shot and people cried in the streets. The year I was born.

The news comes to me over the phone. Each word is banal in itself, but together they shock me breathless.

Someone touches my shoulder. I look up slowly. A nurse. The nurse. In her mid-fifties. She sits down beside me. A gentle voice.

"I'm sorry about your boyfriend."

I don't react.

"He came to around ten in the evening. We talked for a minute or two. He was thirsty. He asked me to write something down for him and give it to you. It wasn't very clear, you know, but I think I got it right."

She hands me a neatly folded piece of paper.

For some reason I am amazed at her handwriting. Nice round clear letters. With the i's precisely dotted and the t's precisely crossed. Incredibly legible. I am awed. Christ, if you compare it with my handwriting, so jagged and half-hysterical.

"Could you keep this a secret, please?" I ask her.

"Sure."

She stands up. She is looking down at me. There is a pause.

Then, just like that, she runs her hand through my hair.

"You poor boy," she says.

2001—After a reign of forty-nine years, Queen Elizabeth II dies. Her reign has witnessed a period of incredible industrial expansion and increasing material prosperity. In its own blinkered and delusional way, the Elizabethan age has been the happiest of all.

Sorry, it's the best I can do. The story is yours.

Paul

The Time I Heard The Private Donald J. Rankin String
Concerto with One Discordant Violin, by the American
Composer John Morton

I was young (I am young; it was last November, November of 1988; I am twenty-five; a student— philosophy) and I was down in Washington, District of Columbia, visiting a high-school friend during a university break. I had never been to the United States before. My friend works in the management-consulting arm of an accounting firm called Price Waterhouse, something to do with their aviation practice, he makes good money, he went to the John F. Kennedy School of Government at Harvard—but the point is, he was busy at work during the day. So I visited Washington. Walked around. Everywhere. Risked my life, some would say. Saw the belly and genitals of the city. I walked up ordinary streets and down dead ends, I visited public toilets and subway stations, I poked my nose into dingy apartment staircases and dirty little backyards, I contemplated plain and ugly buildings, I patronized tacky bars and greasy spoons, I examined sewer grates and traffic jams. I found everything interesting because everything was a part of Washington and Washington was new and foreign to me. Funny how this city, so rich and powerful, capital of the world in a way, looks so poor in parts. Rundown. Whole areas that need paint and fixing up.

I was walking back home along some street when a sign caught my eye. MERRIDEW THEATER. It was printed in an arc across a store window. Some of the letters were partly scratched out. It was more like MER I EW T EA R. In the bottom left-hand corner of the window was a cardboard sign in red and white. Mel's Barbershop. Through the window, in what should have been the theatre, or at least part of it, the box office perhaps, I could see two barber chairs. A black man was sitting in the one closest to me and another black man—Mel?—was cutting his hair. The Merridew Theater, it seemed, was defunct. Ah, but what's this? To the right of the door was a small display case. There was a paper inside. A sign of life? I got closer.

Special Concert at the Merridew Theater
The Maryland Vietnam War Veterans' Chamber Ensemble
plays
Albinoni
Bach
Telemann
and the world première of
The Private Donald J. Rankin String Concerto
with One Discordant Violin, by John Morton
8 p.m. Thursday November 20th 1988
COME ONE, COME ALL
tickets: only $10

That was tomorrow night.

Great. Another aspect of Washington to explore, another convolution in its brain. Not that I was particularly interested in the Vietnam War. It was a foreign war, an American trauma. I had seen the serious movies on it, had read the odd thing or two, I knew it sank Johnson— but the whole thing was alien to me, nearly folkloric, like the Second World War, the stuff of documentaries and hero movies. Nor would I be going for the music, really. I was attracted by the sights, by the *happening* of this Merridew Theater concert, not by the sounds. Although this Rankin Concerto, with One Discordant Violin, whatever that was, was intriguing. I would ask my friend if he wanted to come. I had hardly seen him since I had arrived.

But he was busy. Price Waterhouse was about to close a deal with Texas Air's unions. And the City of New York had responded earlier than expected to a PW proposal to do work at JFK and LaGuardia airports. He was busy.

So there I was the next evening, about twenty to eight, for the socioanthropology of it, in front of the Merridew Theater. I tried the door. It opened. To my left, the door to Mel's place. Straight ahead, a corridor, at the very end of which I could see a paper taped to the wall. I walked down the corridor. THIS WAY said the paper, with an arrow pointing left to a door. I went through.

I was in the lobby of the Merridew Theater. To my right was a series of double glass doors—the front of the theatre. I suppose the doors gave onto another, parallel street, but I couldn't tell: they were all boarded up. Against these doors was a long, rolled-up carpet. I also noticed the ticket booth, a solid, round structure whose windows were amazingly dirty. Clearly, the theatre had been closed down and I had just come in through the back door. I stepped forward. I noticed to my left two men sitting behind a table. They were looking at me. The word "trespassing" flashed in my mind.

"Th-th-there-there *is* a concert here tonight, isn't there?"

"Yes, sir," said the black man.

"Oh. Well, hello. One ticket please."

"That'll be ten dollars."

I gave my ten dollars to the white man in the wheelchair. He put it in the cash box in front of him and gave me a program.

"Am I too early?"

"No. Just pick up a chair over there and sit where you want," replied the black man.

He pointed to a stack of orange, plastic folding chairs. I was certain I had understood him correctly so I walked over and picked one up. I wasn't sure where I was supposed to go. Was the concert outside in a parking lot? Or here in the lobby?

"That way."

This time he was pointing to doors at the back of the lobby.

"Thank you."

As I had a hand on one of the doors, I turned and looked about the lobby.

"Fixing things up?"

"I beg your pardon?"

"Are they reconstructing the theatre?"

"No, they're tearing it down."

"Oh. Thank you."

A furtive operation, this Vets' Ensemble, I thought, as I pushed the door and entered the theatre.

I would have burst out laughing except that there were people. To start with, there wasn't a single fixed seat in the house. Every row had been removed, seemingly torn out without care for the damage done. The effect was of a bizarre series of war trenches: between rows of dark red carpeting ran channels of grey cement, with chipped holes and cement flakes everywhere, and here and there rusted bolts sticking out. The strong, musty smell in the air came from the intricate blotches of yellowish-brown, black-streaked mould that made the walls look like huge, medieval maps. And at the foot of the wall opposite me, between the First World War trenches and the pestiferous towns of the Middle Ages, stretching nearly its entire length, were the remains of Antiquity: a number of smashed, pseudo-Greek plaster sculptures. Arms, legs, heads, torsos, shields—it was a carefully aligned, evenly spaced hecatomb of deities.

I walked into this mess of broken civilizations. The stage had been swept and it was well lit. At the centre of its glow was a crescent of twelve orange seats and twelve stands, with a thirteenth stand in the middle. The arrangement looked neat and tidy. At least art would have a clean space. I unfolded my seat and set it down. After I cleared away a few cement flakes with my foot, it was steady. I examined the program. It was a photocopy job.

The left side:

Tomaso Albinoni: Concerto in B flat, opus 9, No. 1
Concerto in G minor, opus 10, No. 8
Johann Sebastian Bach: Concerto No. 6 in B flat major
Concerto in A minor
Concerto in D minor
Georg Philipp Telemann: Concerto in G major
intermission

*John Morton: The Private Donald J. Rankin String
Concerto with One Discordant Violin
(World Première)*

The right side:

*The Maryland Vietnam
War Veterans' Chamber Ensemble
is
Fritz Hauser; conductor
Joe Slewter; first violin
Fred Cuzo, Peter Davis, Randy Dempster,
Zeb Kerkowsky, John Morton, Calvin Sheen; violins
Stan "Laurel" Mackie, Stu Scott; violas
Lance Gustafson, Luigi Mordi; cellos
Luke Smith; contrabass*

*Special thanks to: Fife, Jeff, Marvin, Frenchie;
Don Beech and the music department
of Morrow Heights Junior High School;
the Mayor's Office, City of Washington, DC;
Dazzlin' Dan; and, especially, for kicking us
when we needed kicking, Billy.*

The back of the program was an ad for Dazzlin' Dan's
Pizzeria.

So the composer of the Rankin Concerto was a member of the ensemble. Interesting. I would have to go to
Dazzlin' Dan's. The address was 249 Dorlin Street. I

folded the program and put it in my breast pocket. I looked about the Merridew again. Unbelievable.

There were maybe 150-odd spectators. Nearly all men. I'd say most were in their late thirties, early forties. Many knew each other. There were plenty of greetings— "Hey, Gary," "Hey, Phil," "Hey, Art," "Hey, Dennis"— before they settled down. I seemed to be the only spectator who was on his own.

At a quarter after eight, the two men from the ticket table came in. The white man, cash box on his lap, wheeled down to the front while the other sat near the doors. All at once the house went dark. Only the stage remained lit.

Thirteen men in tuxedos walked on stage. Immediately there were shouts and cheers, as if we were at a football game. The men smiled, bowed and sat down. I tried to figure out which was John Morton. The violins were seated on the left. I reckoned Joe Slewter, as first violin, was the one in the first seat. Now, do violinists sit in alphabetical order or is there some sort of hierarchy, that was the question. If they sat in alphabetical order, John Morton was white and somewhat overweight, with fat features and long, greased-back hair that curled at the ends. Not very good-looking. Early forties, I'd say. That was violin number six.

The musicians spent a few moments shifting their chairs and adjusting themselves and tuning their instruments.

Fritz Hauser turned to the audience. We fell silent.

He said (and I swear this is an exact quote):

"The fire marshal of Washington, DC, has asked me to ask you to please absolutely totally refrain from smoking."

"What!" somebody shouted. "No joints?!"

Everybody laughed, including Fritz and his ensemble. I was trying to imagine von Karajan saying, "The fire marshal of Berlin has asked me...."

He raised his hands. Silence.

"Albinoni's Concerto in B flat."

He turned around. He raised his left hand. Bows went to strings. A moment of tension. Then his hand dropped—and my ears were invaded.

It was the volume that struck me dumb. One second the Merridew was collapsed in empty silence; the next, it was full of this wonderful, meandering, sliding sound, a sound that penetrated the whole theatre, down to the very last crack and crevice. I am certain that every mouse and cockroach in the place was at attention. And all this produced by those small, brown objects.

I took in the consonance of things: the way the bows moved together, the way the hands climbed up and down the fingerboards like so many spiders, the way Hauser's movements were translated into their musical equivalent, the way Slewter would lead, and then be followed. Such ability, such agility—how do they do it? What would it mean to be able to do that with one's hands?

Albinoni's Concerto in B flat was in three parts.

Unfortunately, I know nothing about music so I cannot describe it properly, but the first part of the concerto was very lively, like a dance. I could imagine couples flying in circles with gorgeous dresses swishing and swooshing. The melody went up and down, up and down, up and down, and then in splendid spirals, and then up and down again, and then it ended. The notes fell off beautifully. The second part was more like a serious, slow-moving straight line, but with a climbing grandeur, as if the line were following the arête of a high mountain where the air is rare and misty. The third part was like the first, with ups and downs and spirals, though maybe a little slower.

Music, what a strange, unique thing it does. Unlike words, sobs, laughter, throats clearing, fingers snapping and what not, music is not a code. There is nothing concrete to understand in it. It is a beautiful nonsense that has little use for the deciphering mind. And so the voice in our head goes quiet. There are no more words. Notes, harmony and tempo become our thinking. The verbal mind has been bypassed.

During the Concerto in B flat, Albinoni did my thinking. I don't recall any words, only a fluctuating flow of melody.

When the concerto ended, the spectators clapped and cheered. The Maryland Vets' Ensemble stood up, bowed and sat down. Up went Hauser's hand and down went Hauser's hand and the music started again, only this time it was Albinoni's Concerto in G minor.

It was lovely too, but I can't remember it that well. The truth is, my attention was starting to wander. Half-way through the concerto, words started cropping up in my mind. I started thinking about Texas Air Corporation. My friend had explained the whole situation to me. Texas Air was based in Houston and its president was a man named Frank Lorenzo. It wasn't an airline company itself—my friend called it a holding company—but it owned two airlines: Eastern and Continental. It seemed Eastern, based in Miami, was experiencing severe financial difficulties. It was embroiled in a dispute with its three unions over wages, retirement benefits and working conditions and was steadily losing customers. To reduce losses and generate cash to finance operations, Texas Air was shrinking the airline by selling assets and trimming its staff and routes. For example, it had sold the profitable New York–to-Boston and New York–to-Washington shuttles to Donald Trump for 365 million dollars. But the unions were claiming that the whole thing was— Claps and cheers. Albinoni was over. A bit stiffly but smiling all the way, the Maryland Ensemble got up, bowed, left the stage, came back and sat down. Up, down, music. I took out the program and read it by the light of the stage. Bach's Concerto No. 6 in B flat major. The first part was led by the violas, Mackie and Scott. It was a swaying, ascending melody that sounded like two climbers tied to a rope: Mackie would move the melody forward, then Scott would catch up and pass him, but then Mackie would redouble his efforts and surge ahead of Scott, who would then … etcetera. The other instruments did background work, the noise at a party that allows two people in a corner to be intimate. But the second part of the concerto was ponderous to my ears and it quickly lost me.…

The unions were claiming that the whole thing was a sham, that the sale of the shuttle routes and the wage-cut demands were all part of Texas Air's plans to dismantle Eastern through bankruptcy, which would allow it to break contracts and slash wages and reconstruct it as a non-union carrier. Lorenzo had done exactly that in 1983 with Continental. The dispute was bitter and protracted, a real war, and the publicity hadn't done Eastern any good. Travel agents were reporting that some customers didn't want Eastern flights even when these were the most convenient. If the dispute went on much longer—a matter of months, some analysts were saying—the airline might no longer— No. 6 slid to an end. Clap clap, cheer cheer, Hauser up, Hauser down, music. The same as before: music, but then my mind started talking. I hardly remember Bach's Concerto in A minor, only that Slewter did a lot of playing.

The whole thing was enormously complicated, but my friend was right into it. PW was trying to get a contract with the unions and every night he brought home piles of documents and worked till two in the morning. During breaks, he would tell me about developments— the good Lorenzo's latest move, some judge's ruling, the grumblings and threats of the AFL-CIO, etc.—and I would tell him where I had been that day, what rundown neighbourhoods I had walked through, how my cheese-burger and fries had been, if I had met anyone nice, if I had seen anything that was both shabby and beautiful.

Merridew. I wondered who Merridew was. Wasn't he the American Secretary of State who bought Alaska from the Russians? No, that was Seward. Seward's Folly it was called, not Merridew's. Does anybody know who Merridew is?

I looked about the theatre. What *was* I doing here? Five days ago I had been in familiar Peterborough, not happy, but not particularly unhappy, just wondering a bit what to make of life—and here I was in Washington, DC, listening to a bunch of Vietnam vets playing Bach in a theatre that looked like Beirut. What should I do, where should I head, I wondered. After a number of interruptions, I would be getting my Bachelor's this coming summer, finally. I considered various career options. In what oyster did I want to be a grain of sand?

Clapping made me realize that the A minor was over. What next? Concerto in D minor. *Olé.* It had some nice violin parts, but I couldn't help thinking. Looking at the program again, I noticed that they had used colons between the composers and their concertos, but semicolons between the musicians and their roles or instruments. Interesting. This reminded me of Joseph Conrad. Conrad has marvellous punctuation. It's never excessive—there are never too many commas or unnecessary suspension dots—and his use of the semicolon and the dash is masterly. There is one example that I'll never forget. It's from Conrad's first novel, *Almayer's Folly*. Almayer has been working in the desolation of a remote corner of the Malay Archipelago for twenty years. He hates it, has hated it all along, but has kept at it because he wants to return to Europe a rich man for his beautiful, half-caste daughter Nina's sake. As he puts it, *I wanted to see white men bowing low before the power of your beauty and your wealth*. But twenty years in the archipelago have been twenty years of disappointment, humiliation and poverty. And finally Nina, who has never known anything but this tropical clime and is happy here, chooses to marry her Malay lover, Dain, in spite of her father's objections. She'll never be going to Europe. Almayer is devastated. He has lost it all, everything, has achieved nothing but ruin. Yet it didn't have to be this way. Almayer feels that time and again he nearly made it. Glory, fortune, success—nearly achieved, nearly, but for some misfortune, some error:

> *He looked at his daughter's attentive face and jumped to his feet upsetting the chair.*
>> *"Do you hear? I had it all there; so; within reach of my hand."*

That is a brilliant use of semicolons. An ordinary writer would have used commas. Dashes would have done the job, but semicolons, by isolating the "so" without making it parenthetical, give the word a physical impact. As the word is read, one naturally imagines a tight fist shaking in the air, one feels the twenty years that have added up to nothing. The punctuation of this sentence is not peripheral or incidental, it is forceful—even theatrical. It is the punctuation of a true master.

D minor was through. When *would* this concert end? What time was it? Only 9:33 p.m. Still the Telemann Concerto in G major to go before intermission. And that was just half the program. The thought of leaving at intermission entered my head. But no; come on, I said to myself, Morton is there, in front of you. And what's a "discordant violin"? It could be very good. I closed my eyes and went about convincing myself of this. I remembered that Dutch violinist I had heard in Montreal. He had played pure unadulterated noise: screeching high notes, endless low notes, frantic plucking. Not a trace of a melody. It was wonderful. An assault on the senses. Full of life. And what about Melnyk, Lubomyr Melnyk? Polish Canadian but living in Sweden but I saw him in Peterborough. He played what he called continuous music. His fingers moved like little waves up and down the piano, the same melody, but not really; it changed ever so slowly, monotonous in a mesmerizing way. Yes, this Rankin Concerto could be very interesting. Why, I wouldn't miss it for anything.

The second part of the Telemann concerto was very energetic. I didn't think. After a flourish, it ended. There was clapping, whistling and hooting. The ensemble members bowed several times and left the stage. The house lit up.

Intermission, finally.

"I GOT MICHELOB, I GOT OLD MILWAUKEE, I GOT CORONA AND I GOT LONE STAR!" It was the black man at the doors. He had produced from I don't know where three big blue coolers. The white man with the cash box quickly wheeled up to him and parked himself behind the coolers. In my Canadian mind I asked myself, "Is this legal?" The two were rapidly surrounded by spectators and a small symphony of *pssshhheeettt* can-opening sounds began. I got up to stretch my legs. I walked through the trenches of Verdun and had a look at the medieval town of, say, Nuremberg, wondering if I would see a burgher bug crawling about the streets. I pulled at a strip of suburb. Glancing down at the Greek morgue, I saw the Goddess of Wisdom. Or rather, what was left of her helmeted head.

The intermission stretched on. I felt like an uninvited guest at a party. I checked my program. No, there was no mistake, it wasn't over. Just a long intermission. I returned to my seat and hunkered down.

Suddenly, I felt it. I felt the tension. The spectators were tense. Most had rejoined their seats and the talking had greatly diminished.

Finally, after close to forty minutes of intermission, Hauser walked on stage, followed by the ensemble. I could hear the creaking of the floor boards. It dawned on me: Albinoni, Bach, Telemann—all time-killers. Every-one was here for the Rankin Concerto.

The lights went out.

The alphabet theory was correct: John Morton was

who I thought he was. He walked over to Hauser and whispered a few words to him. Hauser nodded. Then Morton moved a little to the conductor's left. He brought his violin to his neck and wiped his left hand against his jacket, holding the instrument up with his chin. He lightly ran his fingers over the fingerboard. He lifted his right hand. There wasn't a chair creaking, a cough. He turned to the musicians. He turned to Hauser. Hauser brought his left hand up. Bows hung over strings. Morton had his eyes on the left hand. The hand came down.

How can I describe what I heard?

If music were colour, the theatre would have been a hurricane of colours. I could have described the sombre blue that poured from the contrabass, the blue and green that flowed from the violas and cellos, the yellow and orange that streamed from the violins. And especially, I could have described the red and black that cried from Morton's violin. If music were colour and I were a chameleon, I would have changed colours for ever, I would be indelibly streaked in the colours of the Rankin Concerto.

I could describe the music with my deaf eyes. There was nothing to be seen except the stage. The rot and the decay of the theatre disappeared. The spectators disappeared. Only the stage existed. And on that stage, only John Morton. I saw an ugly man become beautiful. The ugly man had bulging eyes and a piggish face and a belly that strained his rented tuxedo. The beautiful man was crumpled over, disfigured, visibly trembling, hardly controlling his violin. I saw ugliness become suffering become beauty.

The Rankin Concerto wasn't long, not ten minutes, and they didn't do it right, nor did they finish it the way they were supposed to, but never have I been so moved as during those few minutes. Everything in my life that is waste, torment and trivia was swept away. During the Rankin Concerto, I glimpsed the sublime.

It started formally, as I imagine an eighteenth-century court dance might start. Imagine the dancers as they move slowly and precisely, each knowing what to do and what his or her partner will do. Then it tumbled into a lively, logical melody. The notes declined so naturally I could nearly predict them, could imagine completing the concerto if it were left unfinished in my care. The concerto then began to climb in tight spirals to very high notes. It stayed on these high notes through turn after turn, vacillating like a spinning dish at the end of a stick in a Chinese acrobats' show. From that height, it crashed down into the lively melody again, crashed down as a spring torrent crashes down. Imagine transparent water rushing over slippery, moss-covered rocks and exploding against boulders.

Morton carried most of the melody. He would often break away to put out curls of pioneer notes. The ensemble, in hot, slow pursuit, would swell and repeat these notes. The melody was intricate and Morton's left hand jumped and trembled all over the fingerboard while his bow see-sawed frantically. And right from the start, he was making mistakes. This I must make clear, it is capital: the Rankin Concerto was poorly played. Even my ears could detect notes that were smudged or a slowing down in the playing because Morton couldn't keep up. But it didn't detract. The very opposite. The full beauty of the Rankin Concerto was expressed through Morton's inept playing. His every false note hinted at impregnable perfection, his every falter was cathartic. This was like no classical music I had ever heard before. There was no arid precision here; as in all things truly human, it was mostly beauty and error.

The melody slowed down. It didn't stop—Mackie and Scott were producing steady blue notes—but it seemed to be catching its breath, much as Morton was. He wiped his left hand and licked his lips. His expression was strained.

The ensemble revived and played deep, tugging undernotes.

Morton started to play again. Here my tricks of communication will fail me. I wish I knew something about music. There are probably technical terms that define precisely what Morton did, but if there are, I don't know them. How does one say in the dry language of music teaching that my soul was pulled out of me and was up there, in the air, attached to each note? How does one say that I breathed, that I existed, to the ups and downs of those notes? And what kind of notes are they that gyre and waver about, one moment trembling, seemingly about to disappear, the next clawing at the air wildly, each one, flawed or perfect, of a delicacy that hurt me? What kind of notes are both elevating and crushing?

In the midst of this blessed suffering came the discordant violin. It didn't last thirty seconds. The ensemble was producing a large body of blue, green and orange middle notes, hovering notes, when Morton suddenly began playing, above and below them, high red notes and low black notes. This alternating was stunning. I have no words for it. It was sound, as if I had been deaf until then. It was an outburst of terrible grief, like a child's grief, throbbing and overwhelming, that reverberates in every corner of the universe. For those few seconds, I beheld agony in its full panoply of meaning.

The discordant violin ended with the whole ensemble playing the same uniform, oscillating notes. It was an abrupt break, like a sudden gaining of control. But Morton was hardly in control—he was making mistakes continually—and then he wasn't at all. He stopped playing. He let his hands, one holding the violin, the other the bow, drop to his sides. The rest of the ensemble lost control too. The melody was there; it began to stray; then it was lost completely. The ensemble became eleven colourblind musicians playing nothing but errors. They gave up the struggle and the silence was sudden. Hauser stood with his hands covering his face.

I felt as though I had been let go, as though I had fallen back into myself on my seat. My heart was pounding and I was breathing through my mouth and I wanted to bring my hand out, towards him, Morton, in appeal. It was there! It was there! I had seen it, I had felt it! Great, omnipotent beauty.

The silence lasted. Emotion was on the surface of everything. I felt that if I touched the walls, they would quiver.

I became aware of various sounds. Bodies moving in chairs. Sudden, measured respirations. Still, no one got up. Morton was looking into space.

Finally, the spectators began to leave. Quietly. As if we were in a church. The members of the ensemble disappeared off stage. Morton was the third to go. The Merridew, beautiful for a few minutes, became a ruin again.

I didn't move. I can't remember now what I was thinking, but for several minutes I felt that the walls to my ways of thinking had been pulled down and I experienced an amazing feeling of freedom. I felt empty; open; re-created.

The lights came on. I was alone. I didn't move.

The black man came in. He noisily started stacking the orange chairs, oblivious of me. I decided to help him. After stacking about fifteen chairs and feeling that I had earned a bit of conversation, I said, choking on it somewhat, "That was beautiful."

He stacked two more chairs before replying. "Yep."
I stacked another ten. "Has he recorded anything?"
"Nope."
Another ten. "Has he composed anything else?"
"Nope. Only time he got his act together."

We finished stacking the chairs. "Is he married?"

A stupid question. I don't know why I asked it. It was the first question I could think of that wasn't related to music.

"Is he *married?*" he repeated, looking at me for the first time. "Yeah, he's married. Her name's Johnnie Walker."

Definitely not a friendly man. I looked about the theatre one last time. "See you," I said.

"Yep."

I passed through the swinging doors.

At the table in the lobby, the white man in the wheelchair was counting money. He looked up and nodded. I waited till he had finished counting a stack of ten-dollar bills.

"That was beautiful," I said.

"Yeah, wasn't it." He smiled and nodded again. He had a veiled Southern accent. "But I wished they'd finished it."

"Well, I thought it was great like that."

"Oh yeah, I agree with you totally. It was great like that too."

"Has he composed anything else?"

"Oh yeah, lots of stuff. But nothing quite as finished as this. You know, he really finished this one. Completely."

He started counting a stack of five-dollar bills.

"Make a good profit?"

"*Profit?* You're dreaming, my man. We should just

about have enough to cover the tuxedos and the chairs."

"Really. Do you always play here?"

"No, usually we play in this high school auditorium, but this time we decided to go for a real theatre, what with John's concerto. That was the world première, you know."

"Yeah, I read that. You should try to get it recorded somewhere. A radio station maybe. Somewhere, anyway. I mean, it was really something."

"Yeah, we should. But it's tough, you know, it's tough. We've tried before. But Billy's going to try again, probably."

He started counting a stack of dollar bills. There were footsteps behind. I turned. It was John Morton. I know this is silly, but I could feel myself blushing. I had seen him on stage, up there, removed, but to have him here, in front of me—I was dumbstruck. It was like that time I saw Neil Armstrong in Ottawa when I was fourteen. He was attending a scientific conference. I saw him under the porch of the Château Laurier while he was waiting for his car. I was fascinated by the space program. I read books about it, I had posters of the Apollo crews, I had all kinds of models; best of all, I had this LP record that related the story of the Apollo 11 lunar mission, using the real voices. Even now, when I put on that record, my heart pounds when I hear the first words from the moon, when I hear Buzz Aldrin say, "Houston. This is the Sea of Tranquility. The Eagle has landed." I hear those words and I dream for hours. Aldrin had a rough time later on, problems with alcohol, but I'm sure he never regretted anything. The Day I Saw Neil Armstrong—it's one of the important stories I tell when I make new friends. If they don't react well, I hold it against them. If they also don't react well when I tell them Gerard Manley Hopkins is one of my favourite poets, I usually downgrade these new friends to the rank of acquaintances. People who don't share the same poetics can't be real friends.

John Morton was dressed in baggy green workpants and a shirt to match. The shirt collar had big, worn tips. He was holding a violin case in one hand and a plastic bag in the other. He looked drawn. I moved aside and stared at his big face and at his violin case. I had a vision that the case contained a small brown animal, very aggressive and dangerous except in the hands of its trainer.

"Hi, Fife."

Morton had a light accent, not very far from a Canadian one. Fife stopped counting.

"Hey, John. Great concert, man, great concert."

Morton shrugged.

"Really. I was just talking about it. It was great, wasn't it?" Fife looked at me.

"Yeah, it was. I've never heard anything like it. It was incredible." I stammered a bit, but it still came out clearly.

"But I couldn't finish it."

"We were just saying it was beautiful like that. Didn't matter," Fife replied.

I nodded vigorously.

Morton shook his head. "Can I give you this?" He held up the bag. Sly Sy, it said. With a picture of a fox dressed in a tuxedo on it.

"Yeah, sure." Fife took the bag and opened it. "Everything's in there?"

"Yeah."

"Good." Fife dropped the bag beside his wheelchair. There were already several there.

"Okay. Thanks. I gotta run." Morton half-turned and passed his right hand through his hair.

"John, it was great," said Fife again.

Morton nodded. "Where's Billy?"

Fife pointed at the swinging doors.

"What's he doing?"

"Probably destroying the chairs."

Morton smiled wearily. "What did *he* think?"

"Well," said Fife in a long drawl, "at one point I thought he was going to rip off my right wheel, so I guess he liked it."

"Really?" said Morton.

"John, trust me. That's the way it should be—so beautiful you can't finish it."

Morton liked that. He cracked a hesitant smile. "Okay. Gotta run. Meeting tomorrow, right?"

"As usual."

"Okay. Night, Fife. Thanks."

"See you tomorrow, Johnny boy."

Morton nodded to me, turned and walked off. I

watched him go. Fife started counting change. Did I dare or didn't I? It was too late. No it wasn't. It was. It wasn't. Suddenly I made my mind up.

"I have to go. Good-night. I thought it was an amazing concert. In fact, best concert I've ever been to. Really, I mean that sincerely."

"Thanks a lot."

"Okay, bye."

"Bye."

I pushed the door and raced down the corridor. Just as I got to the street, I saw Morton in a car pulling away from the curb and heading to my right. It was an enormous, rectangular box of a car that made a noise like a tugboat. I started running after it like a madman.

It's not that I do this sort of thing a lot, but thanks to red lights, slow turning, dirty sparkplugs and hard running, I managed to follow Morton all the way to where he was going, which seemed like miles. I don't know what cut-throat neighbourhoods I sprinted through. When I got to Morton's parked car, he was nowhere in sight. Gasping for breath, I collapsed on the sidewalk. I was drenched in sweat, my heart was jumping around in my chest and my leg muscles were aching. "Christ, all this effort for nothing."

After several minutes, I started feeling better. I walked around the car slowly. Where could he be? Where did he live?

Then I saw him. Across the street. A bank. It was closed, obviously, but there were some lights still on, lights that were left on all night. Morton was walking in front of the counters. He was pushing a cart that had trays full of cleaning products, brushes and rags.

A *janitor*?

He pushed the cart to the middle of the floor and took out a Mr. Clean bottle. He drank two gulps from it. Then he began to sweep the marble floor with a broom, a flat, soft, orange thing. When he had finished, he pushed the cart against the counters and disappeared to the right.

He reappeared after a minute with one of those heavy floor-polishing machines with a flat, round buffing pad in the front and two small wheels in the back. He proceeded to polish the floor in a slow, to-and-fro motion. I couldn't hear the machine, but I knew it made a moderately loud humming sound.

What did I have to say to this man? All I wanted to do was give him a heartfelt compliment. But might he not take it wrong? Might he not find me annoying, think that I was being condescending? Morton took two breaks to drink from the Mr. Clean bottle. If he got drunk, he might get belligerent—or talkative.

Soon enough he had polished the entire floor.

I had to make a decision. Quickly. It was late, dark, I'd come this far—it would be....

I crossed the street, stepped up to the window and knocked on the glass.

Morton turned. His puzzled, fat face was on me. He looked a second, then turned away.

I knocked once more.

He turned a second time. I pointed to my right, to the doors.

He turned his palms out and shrugged.

I brought out my left hand and raised my right hand in the air and played an imaginary violin.

He got closer to the window. I pointed to the doors and to my mouth and to him. *Talk.*

He pointed to his wrist. *Do you know what time it is?*

I shrugged. I played the violin again.

He nodded.

But didn't move. I played the violin and then I bunched my fingers together in front of me, shook them for a second and then released them. *It was great.*

He nodded. And pointed to his right, my left. The doors were the other way.

We walked side by side. We turned the corner—of the sidewalk for me, of the bank for him. He was heading for a door and pointed at me to keep walking beyond the end of the windows. I arrived in front of a glass door the lower half of which was glazed. When Morton hit a light switch, I could see that it opened onto a corridor. He came up to the door.

He looked at me.

He wet the tip of his finger and began writing on the glass door. I figured out that he was writing "Merridew".

I nodded, wet my finger and wrote "Rankin".

He nodded. He wrote a huge question mark and pointed at me.

I wrote a huge exclamation mark and pointed at him. He looked at me.

I shrugged. *Why not?*

He pulled from his pocket a keychain with about ten keys on it. He introduced a key into a keyhole in the wall and turned it a quarter. Then he unlocked the door. It had three deadbolts, each requiring a different key. I prepared myself. The door opened.

"Listen," I said, "I just want to tell you that your concerto was fantastic, amazing, took my breath away, didn't expect anything like it, that discordant violin, it was —"

"I can't keep the door open like this. Come on in."

I stepped in quickly. "Thank you. But I don't want to bother you."

"It's all right."

He locked the door again and turned the key in the wall back a quarter.

"I like the discordant violin too," he added.

"I've never heard anything like it. And the rest of the concerto too. Most beautiful thing I've ever heard in my life."

Morton smiled. He wasn't looking at me.

"Great, great. Uh … listen, I have to work. We can talk while I'm working. Are your shoes clean?"

"Yes."

I wiped them hard against the carpet. We walked across the polished floor.

"Have you composed much else?"

"Oh, yeah. Lots of stuff, lots of stuff. Here, do you

want to clean the phones for me? While we're talking? I'll
show you how."

"Sure, I'd love to."

He took a cloth and a white plastic bottle from the
cart. I followed him behind the counters.

"You do it like this. You squirt the cloth with some of
this." It smelt of alcohol. He picked up a phone. "Then
you wipe the body, the cradle—you push down on the
plunger, you don't try to clean around it—then the but-
tons. Then you do the handset. You really wipe the
mouthpiece. Bank people spit a lot. Then you take the
handset with your cloth and put it back, wiping it just a
bit more so there aren't any fingerprints. That way, they
don't know you've been cleaning after them. Okay?"

"Got it."

There are a lot of phones in a bank. Morton fetched a
bottle of Windex and a clean rag and began cleaning the
panes between the tellers' booths. It occurred to me:
you're in Washington, it's the middle of the night, you're
in a bank, you're with Mozart and you're cleaning phones.

"You should try getting your concerto recorded by a
radio station."

"They don't take non-professional stuff."

"Oh." I had never thought of that.

"So was Donald Rankin a friend of yours?" I was wiping this mouthpiece so hard I'm surprised the handset
didn't break into two pieces.

"Yeah, he was."

I finished the phones. "You want me to do the desks?"

"Sure." He got me another rag, a soft cotton one. "You're just dusting. If you move or lift anything, make sure you put it back exactly where it was. Especially papers. Okay?"

"Yep."

There are a lot of desks in a bank.

He went over to do the panes on the other side.

"You know, I wish I had finished it." Because he was on the other side, he spoke louder. "On our own, we can play it, no problems. But in public, in front of everybody, I get so nervous. All those damn mistakes. I wanted it to be perfect."

"But really," I replied, "as Fife said, it didn't matter. Your thing was...." I couldn't find the words. I waved my hands about, as if this turned them into powerful adjectives.

"Still, I wish we had finished it."

He finished the panes. He came over and helped me with the desks. "You know," he continued, "at least you feel Bach is a part of it all. You feel that if he were taken away, some things would collapse. Me? What do I do? Sometimes I feel like I just make a *leisure* product, the sort of thing you relax with after the serious part of life, after the earning of money. Like I'm some sort of small-time rival of Atari or Mattel. Small-time—Christ, not even that. You know, I've been working here for eleven years. I put up a poster at the door, with my name underlined. Do you think any of these bank people came? Sometimes it feels like a waste of life, I tell you. Here, I'll get the vacuum cleaner."

He walked to the polishing machine, pushed down on its handles and rolled it away to the left. He came back with a vacuum cleaner. I was expecting something big and industrial, looking like a barrel maybe, but it was this tiny thing on three wheels with a very long cord. Morton plugged it in.

"Vacuum cleaners are like dogs," he said. "The smaller they are, the louder."

He turned it on. Indeed. This chihuahua of a vacuum cleaner made a noise like a Rolls-Royce airplane engine.

"YOU MOVE—" Morton shouted. He turned it off. "You move the chairs and wastepaper baskets and I'll vacuum, okay?"

I nodded and he turned it on again. The way the thing was sucking, I was amazed it didn't eat the carpet pile and just leave the burlap. I rolled the chairs about and lifted the wastepaper baskets.

There's a lot of carpeting in a bank.

Morton started talking to me. He didn't seem to mind having to shout. In fact, I think he was glad of the background noise and of the effort he had to make.

"I READ IN A MAGAZINE ONCE ABOUT THIS CHOREOGRAPHER. HE LAUGHED, *LAUGHED*, AT PEOPLE WHO THOUGHT DANCE WAS JUST ENTERTAINMENT. HE SAID DANCE WAS A PHILOSOPHY. I LIKE THAT. A *PHILOSOPHY*." He vacuumed in clean, easy sweeps. "YOU KNOW WHERE I WAS HAPPIEST WITH MY MUSIC? YOU WANT ME TO TELL YOU?"

Yesyesyes, I nodded.

"WAY BACK IN VIETNAM. I WENT OVER WHEN I WAS NINETEEN, JUST OUT OF HIGH SCHOOL. I GOT THERE IN OCTOBER OF 1967. I'D TAKEN MUSIC IN HIGH SCHOOL. I COULD READ AND WRITE IT ALL RIGHT. SO I GOT THERE AND WHERE DID I END UP IN JANUARY? *KHE SANH.* HAVE YOU HEARD OF KHE SANH? WELL, YOU KNOW IN THE MIDDLE AGES HOW THEY USED TO SURROUND CASTLES AND HOLD THEM IN SIEGE? THAT WAS KHE SANH. A SIEGE. ALL THOSE GREAT MODERN WEAPONS, BUT IT WAS LIKE IN THE MIDDLE AGES. WE WERE SUR-ROUNDED SOLID BY THE VIET CONGS. FUCKING WESTMORELAND SAID WE'D BE ALL RIGHT, BUT THE THING LASTED SIX MONTHS. SIX MONTHS SURROUNDED BY PEOPLE WHO SHOT AT YOU AND MORTARED YOU EVERY DAY. SIX FUCKING MONTHS. THAT'S WHERE I MET DON RANKIN. YOU KNOW WHERE HE WAS FROM? MOSCOW MILLS, MISSOURI. CAN YOU *BELIEVE* IT? HERE WE WERE FIGHTING THE VC'S AND THIS GUY COMES FROM A PLACE CALLED *MOSCOW* MILLS. WE PRACTICALLY SHOT HIM WHEN HE TOLD US THAT. I STILL LAUGH ABOUT IT NOW. MOSCOW MILLS, MISSOURI. I'VE BEEN THERE, ACTUALLY." He leaned on the vacuum-cleaner pipe as if it were a cane. "I'M SO GLAD WEST-MORELAND LOST THAT TRIAL WITH CBS. HE WAS AN ASSHOLE AND A LIAR." He started vacuuming again. "ANYWAY, I'D WRITE LETTERS HOME AND

THERE WERE SO MANY THINGS I WANTED TO SAY. BUT I COULDN'T SAY THEM. I'D TRIP OVER MY WORDS AND GET BOGGED DOWN. MAN, MY SENTENCES WERE SO CLOGGED THEY NEEDED DRAINS. AND I DIDN'T WANT TO SCARE MY PARENTS OR MY SISTER. SO FOR THE HELL OF IT I STARTED WRITING DOWN THE SONGS I HEARD OVER THE RADIO. I'D WRITE DOWN THE LYRICS TOO, BUT OFTEN I'D CHANGE THEM AND WRITE MY OWN. DO YOU KNOW WHAT ELVIS PRESLEY SOUNDS LIKE ON THE VIOLIN? OR MOTOWN? OR THE MAMAS AND PAPAS? I USED TO LOVE PLAYING 'MONDAY, MONDAY'." He had a big grin. "I MANAGED TO GET A VIOLIN IN SAIGON. THAT'S WHAT I TOOK IN HIGH SCHOOL, THE VIOLIN. THANK GOD I HAD IT AT KHE SANH. SO I USED TO WRITE DOWN THESE SONGS AND SEND THEM TO MY PARENTS. TO TELL THEM I WAS ALL RIGHT AND ALIVE AND DOING SOMETHING. THEY CAN'T READ MUSIC, BUT THEY'D READ THE LYRICS LIKE THEY WERE LETTERS. WHOLE THING WAS KIND OF DUMB I SUPPOSE, BUT THAT'S WHAT I DID. THEN I GOT TIRED OF BUSTING MY HEAD LISTENING TO A RADIO TRYING TO FIGURE OUT THE KEY AND THE NOTES. I WANTED TO DO SOMETHING MORE—HOW CAN I PUT IT?—MORE REMOVED, SOMETHING AWAY FROM ALL THIS SHIT IN VIETNAM. SO I STARTED WRITING MY OWN STUFF. I PUT EVERYTHING INTO IT. THE GUYS USED TO SAY IT DROVE THEM CRAZY, THAT I WAS WORSE THAN THE

VC'S, BUT ACTUALLY THEY LOVED IT. I REMEMBER WILBUR WAS PLUCKING MY VIOLIN ONCE—HE WAS ANOTHER FRIEND—AND HE SNAPPED A STRING. YOU SHOULD HAVE SEEN HIM. I MEAN, I HAD EXTRA STRINGS, IT WAS NO PROBLEM. BUT HE WAS SO SORRY I THOUGHT HE WAS GOING TO HANG HIM-SELF WITH THE STRING. YOU KNOW WHAT HE DID? HE WAS A RADIO OPERATOR. I DON'T KNOW HOW HE MANAGED IT, BUT THE NEXT AIR-DROP DELIV-ERY HAD ENOUGH STRINGS TO FIT AN ENTIRE VIO-LIN SECTION. YEAH, THEY USED TO SAY IT DROVE THEM CRAZY, BUT I NEVER GOT A SINGLE COM-PLAINT. I'D START PLAYING—AND I'M NOT TALKING YEHUDI MENUHIN HERE, I'M TALKING A FUCKING NINETEEN-YEAR-OLD WHO TOOK VIOLIN IN HIGH SCHOOL. I'D START PLAYING AND IMMEDIATELY, IF THERE WAS A RADIO ON NEARBY, IT WOULD BE TURNED OFF. SHIT, THOSE WERE THE DAYS. THAT'S ANOTHER SONG I USED TO LOVE PLAYING. 'THOSE WERE THE DAYS'. MARY HOPKIN. YOU KNOW IT?" He stopped vacuuming and started singing. I couldn't hear him at all. "GREAT SONG. SO WHEN THINGS WERE CALM AND IT WASN'T RAINING, I'D SIT OUTSIDE WITH MY BACK TO THE BUNKER AND I'D SLOWLY PUT TOGETHER THESE VIOLIN PIECES. I'D WRITE THEM DOWN ON LINED PAPER THAT WILBUR GOT ME. THAT'S WHERE I WAS HAPPIEST WITH MY MUSIC. KHE SANH. I KNEW THEN THAT EVERY-THING ELSE WAS A WASTE OF TIME AND LIFE. I'VE

KNOWN A LOT OF THAT SINCE. WASTED TIME, I MEAN. HAVE I EVER."

We'd finished. He turned the vacuum cleaner off.

"Have I ever," he repeated.

He unplugged the cord and wrapped it around the handle.

"You want a drink?"

"No thanks."

He walked over and picked out the Mr. Clean bottle.

"They don't allow it, sooooo…," he said, with a smile, a sad sort of smile. He took a gulp.

A minute went by. Morton seemed deep in thought. He held Mr. Clean by the neck and swung him gently.

"Fuck, I wish we'd played it right," he said quietly.

"You'll have to play it again some other time."

"Yeah," he replied, flatly.

I couldn't get through to him. I mean, I would take all the alcohol, loneliness and wasted time in the world to have created something as perfectly beautiful. I suppose it's easier saying that than living it, but still, but still.

He stood looking into space.

"Yeah, Donald Rankin was a friend of mine," he said. He took a sudden, deep breath. "I'll put the vacuum cleaner away." He disappeared with it.

"I've been working here for eleven years," he said when he came back. "Lousy job. But it pays the bills and nobody bothers me. There's only one part of my job I enjoy. It's the last thing I do when I finish down here. It's something I always check. One, two, three."

He was pointing at three desks.

"It's mostly women who work here."

He pulled open the top left drawer of one of the desks. At the back, it had a plastic tray full of assorted stationery. Morton slid the tray to the front. Beneath were envelopes with the bank's logo.

"There." Morton pointed. Tucked in beside the envelopes. Hardly visible.

A tampon.

He went to another desk. Another drawer. "There." Another tampon.

A third desk. A third drawer. A third tampon.

"There are more women here than that, but the others don't leave any in their desks. Or maybe they do, but in the locked drawers. Or maybe they just keep them in their purses. I don't know."

He carefully took out the third tampon. Its wrapping paper was worn and wrinkled.

"These things are the only signs of life in this place. I see one of these and I think, 'Blood ... sex ... children ... love.' I remember once I saw this graffiti on a wall in Philadelphia: "I am magical: I can bleed for five days and not die." Isn't that wonderful? Everything else in this bank is dead. Dead and bloodless. I hate this place. I hate it because whenever I come here, I like it, and nearly fall for it. It's comfortable and warm, the people are nice—I say to myself, 'Hey, man, you should get a daytime job here. The pay's good, better than what you make now anyway, you work with people, the hours are sane, hey, why not? *Relax,* take the easy road.' Then I catch myself. This place is so insidious. It crawls up on you quietly … you slowly get used to it, the routine, you know … then you think it's normal … finally you think there's nothing else. Sometimes when I think I've wasted my life and I'm scared about it, I come here during the day and I look in from the outside and I feel better. I think these lives are even more wasted than mine. Why don't they ask for more, I wonder. There used to be a fourth desk. But about a year ago the tampon disappeared. I thought that was great. A surprise. "How annoying," she must have thought. "Damn fertility." But then I emptied the wastepaper basket and I found the saddest thing. I found the tampon. Unused. It had been bent in two, wrapped in a paper and thrown away. Really sad. The next day, I made an effort and got up early and got here before the bank closed. At the desk I saw a woman in her early fifties. Laura Drooks."

He pointed to a desk. There was a grey plastic sign with black letters.

"I didn't speak to her. I just looked at her while pretending to read some pamphlets. She smiled sometimes when people spoke to her, but mostly she had this serious, at-work expression. But I thought she looked sad. A private drama in a public place. I've written something about her. The Laura Drooks Concerto. I name all my pieces after people. It helps me focus. It's a concerto in two movements for flute, violin and orchestra. I'll be finished soon."

He put the tampon back exactly where it had been before, turning and nudging it till he was satisfied.

"Yeah, soon. I'm going to get down to it."

Morton looked about. He looked at the clock on the wall. It was well past one in the morning.

"Well, listen, I have a ton of offices to clean still, you know, back there and upstairs, and you're not really supposed to be here...."

"Hey, no problem. I didn't mean to bother you. I should be getting home anyway."

We walked across the polished floor to the corridor.

"Here, I'll show you where I always work."

We turned right. The third door on the left. He opened it and turned the light on. It was a plain, ordinary office: a chair, a desk, two chairs in front of it, a bland, pastel-coloured reproduction on the wall of a sailing-boat at sea.

"Before work, or during, or after, whenever I feel like it, I come in here and I work. I have a music stand in my locker. I don't know why I chose this office. There are bigger and nicer ones. Just habit, I guess."

"Is this where you wrote the Rankin Concerto?"

"Well, not really. Mostly I brought it together here. You know, finished it, polished it. I actually wrote the Rankin years ago. But I've written a lot of other stuff here."

He paused.

"I like this office. I'm happy here."

He turned the light off.

"So that's where Ludwig van Morton works," he said. And laughed. A dry sort of cackle.

We walked to the glass door.

"Well, listen, I'm glad you liked my concerto. I appreciate that."

"It was extraordinary. I'll never forget it."

"That's great, that's great."

He turned the lock in the wall and unlocked the door.

"It was an honour meeting you, Mister Morton." It came out a bit awkwardly, but I meant it.

"Right. Thanks for helping me clean."

We shook hands.

I was outside. He was holding the door open.

"Next time I come down I'll check if you're playing again."

"Yeah, you do that. We try to play three, four times a year."

"I'll check for sure."

"Yeah, great, thanks. Bye."

"Bye."

He closed and locked the door and turned the alarm system on again. Just before turning away, he smiled and waved at me.

I walked to the other side of the street so he wouldn't see me. He crossed the polished floor, took hold of the cart and disappeared.

That was it, the last I saw of John Morton. My words had been so stubby.

When I got home—it was late, close to two-thirty—

my friend was still up. He was in an expansive mood. His evening had been productive. His desk was a mess of reports read and notes written. It struck me then how many parallel hours there are. There were my hours and there were his hours. He asked me how my concert had been. I didn't know what to say. For some reason, at that moment, I didn't want to mention the name John Morton or the discordant violin. I had a sudden urge to cry, but I just took a deep breath. I said my concert had been "good". My friend expressed surprise. "I've never even heard of the Merridew Theater." I smiled. He told me the latest about Eastern. I asked several questions.

The first thing I did the next morning was go to the Vietnam War Memorial. It's strangely moving. Shaped like a wedge, with the names of the war dead incised in the black marble, it's a tactile memorial: you can touch, you are supposed to touch, the names. After a long search, I found him. There he was. Private Donald J. Rankin. I touched his name gently. Then I moved away and I wept over this stupid war that had nothing to do with me and that I know so little about.

This was some months ago. It's now the summer of 1989. I imagine Hauser and his gang have played once or twice since I saw them. Perhaps they've played the Laura Drooks Concerto for Flute, Violin and Orchestra.

For a while I told people about the concert at the Merridew. But I wasn't pleased with the reactions I got. At first I spoke of "the composer John Morton". This drew blank faces so I enlarged: "the American composer John Morton". Still it wasn't enough. I could tell that what was needed was: "an American composer called John Morton". But this struck me as humiliating. As if you have to say "an Austrian composer called Wolfgang Mozart" to be understood. Now I stick to Armstrong and Hopkins to make friends and I pretty well keep John Morton to myself.

My friend has moved from Washington, DC. He still works for Price Waterhouse, but in New York now. We haven't written in several months.

Eastern Airlines has gone bankrupt. The affair is still going on, but I've stopped reading about it. Last I read, Peter Ueberroth, the man who organized the 1984 L.A. Olympics, was getting involved.

I was accepted into law school recently. I don't want to be a lawyer, but a law degree is a good springboard, I'm told. Springboard to what? I'm bright—people tell me that—but I can't focus. I'm restless.

I'm terrified that one day I'll be working some-where—tie, desk, office, female secretary and all—and I'll look up and I'll see a poorly dressed man eyeing me from the outside, and from his expression I'll know that he's thinking, "Why doesn't he ask for more?"

I'm terrified that late one evening, perhaps after relating an unlikely anecdote about a musical janitor, I'll stumble to my feet upsetting a chair and I'll hear myself shout, "Do you hear? I had it all there; so; within reach of my hand."

Manners of Dying

Manner
of
Dying 8

Dear Mrs. Barlow,

As director of Cantos Correctional Institution and
pursuant to the Right-to-Information law, I am writing
to inform you of how your son Kevin faced up to his
execution by hanging for the crimes he committed.

For his last supper, Kevin ordered: vegetable soup
with crackers; turkey (white meat only) with gravy; peas,
carrots and potatoes; a salad with a Caesar dressing; red
wine; cheesecake. He did not touch any of it.

Kevin did not avail himself of the services of Father Preston.

Periodic checks throughout the evening and night seemed to indicate that Kevin was agitated and did not sleep at all. He was seen pacing about his cell, sitting on his bed, and holding himself up to the window by his fingers to look out.

At 6 a.m., when Father Preston's services were offered again, Kevin asked to see him. What transpired between them is protected by the code of ethics concerning professional secrets and is known only by Father Preston and the Almighty.

At 6:50 a.m., when I entered Kevin's cell with the attending personnel, I found Kevin standing on the far side of the cell beneath the window with Father Preston at his side. I would describe your son as: pale and frightened. I read him the judgment concerning his execution as handed down by the legal and legitimate courts of the land in accordance with the law, informed him that I was here to carry out this judgment and asked him if he understood this. Kevin did not react, but I believe he understood me. I asked him to accompany me. Because of his trembling, he seemed incapable of moving and two guards gently, I assure you, assisted him.

As we walked down the corridor, Kevin had difficulty staying on his feet and required the continued assistance of the guards. He also seemed to have trouble with his breathing, which increased when he caught sight of the gallows.

Doctor Lowe assured Kevin that the execution would be painless, which it is. Kevin grabbed hold of the doctor's arm and in a voice that was barely understandable, it was so quavering, he asked him how he knew this. Doctor Lowe explained that the snapping of the neck is so quick, so instantaneous, that the loss of consciousness is immediate and there is no time for pain. Doctor Lowe firmly assured Kevin that he would feel no physical pain.

Kevin's medical file indicated that he was a smoker so I offered him a last cigarette. He took it in his hand, but he did not bring it to his mouth. I told Kevin he had a minute to collect and compose himself and offered him a chair. He sat down and stared at the ground.

After the minute, I asked Kevin if he had any last words or any last message he wished to have transmitted. Out of breath and with great difficulty of articulation, he said: "Tell my mother I love her." I assured him that I would tell you. He tried to speak again, but he was overcome with such a stutter that it was impossible, in spite of all my efforts, to understand him.

As I always do, and insist upon doing, I shook hands with Kevin and wished him, on my own personal behalf, farewell.

Mister Rothway and the guards conveyed Kevin to the gallows and made him stand over the trap. Mister Rothway tied his hands behind his back, covered his head with a hood and put the noose around his neck.

Kevin relieved himself in his pants.

At 7:01 a.m., the trap was released and your son Kevin died painlessly.

Please believe that I share in your grief.

Yours truly,

Harry Parlington
Director,
Cantos Correctional Institution

HP:ym

Manner
of
Dying 13

Dear Mrs. Barlow,

As director of Cantos Correctional Institution and
pursuant to the Right-to-Information law, I am writing
to inform you of how your son Kevin faced up to his
execution by hanging for the crimes he committed.

For his last supper, Kevin ordered: boiled potatoes.
He ate only one potato, but he asked that the plate be
left for the night so he could eat when he wanted.

Father Preston stayed with Kevin for forty-one
minutes. What transpired between them is protected by

the code of ethics concerning professional secrets and is known only by Father Preston and the Almighty.

Periodic checks throughout the evening and night seemed to indicate that Kevin was calm. He was seen pacing about his cell and holding himself up to the window by his fingers to look out. At approximately 1 a.m., Kevin lay down on his bed, covered himself with his blanket and apparently fell asleep.

At 6:03 a.m., I was informed that Kevin was dead. I had Doctor Lowe called immediately.

Kevin took his own life. The autopsy confirmed that he died of asphyxiation after forcing down his throat a potato dropped into one of his socks. The estimated time of death was between 1 a.m. and 3 a.m.

This is not the way I would have had it (none of this is the way I would have had it), but that Kevin chose to do this, on his own terms and in his own time, can perhaps be a comfort to you.

Please believe that I share in your grief.

Yours truly,

Harry Parlington
Director,
Cantos Correctional Institution

HP:ym

Manner
of
Dying 19

Dear Mrs. Barlow,

As director of Cantos Correctional Institution and
pursuant to the Right-to-Information law, I am writing
to inform you of how your son Kevin faced up to his
execution by hanging for the crimes he committed.

For his last supper, Kevin ordered: half an avocado
with a Thousand Island dressing; salmon with a lemon-
butter sauce; carrots and potatoes; Australian white
wine; raspberry ice-cream. He did not touch any of it
except for the ice-cream, of which he asked for seconds.

Father Preston stayed with Kevin for sixteen minutes. What transpired between them is protected by the code of ethics concerning professional secrets and is known only by Father Preston and the Almighty.

Periodic checks throughout the evening and night seemed to indicate that Kevin was very agitated and did not sleep at all. He was seen pacing about his cell frantically, muttering to himself and holding himself up to the window by his fingers to look out.

At 6 a.m., when Father Preston's services were offered again, Kevin did not respond.

At 6:18 a.m., Kevin was heard to start laughing. He laughed continuously, stopping only to catch his breath. I was informed of this and had Doctor Lowe called. Kevin only laughed harder when the doctor offered him tranquillizers. Doctor Lowe ascribed this laughing to psychological stress.

At 6:50 a.m., when I entered Kevin's cell with the attending personnel, I found Kevin sitting on his bed laughing; in fact, laughing even harder at the sight of me. I would describe your son as: very flushed and hysterically agitated. In spite of his laughing, I read Kevin the judgment concerning his execution as handed down by the legal and legitimate courts of the land in accordance with the law, informed him that I was here to carry out this judgment and asked him if he understood this. He only laughed. I became concerned about Kevin's sanity. I asked Doctor Lowe if Kevin could be considered legally insane and if therefore the

legality of his execution could be put into doubt.
Doctor Lowe told me that it was his professional
opinion that Kevin was not insane but merely highly
stressed. I asked Kevin to accompany me. He continued
laughing and did not move. Kevin offered a bit of resistance to the guards — no more than pulling his arms
away and turning — but then he complied. I assure
you there was no violence.

As we walked down the corridor, Kevin kept
bending over to catch his breath and had difficulty
keeping his balance. He required the continued assistance of the guards. When he caught sight of the
gallows, Kevin doubled his laughter, if that is possible. I
became concerned in view of the extreme redness of his
face, the tears flowing from his eyes and his painful
gasps for breath, but Doctor Lowe told me that there
was nothing that could be done at this stage and that it
was not dangerous, the worst that could happen being a
fainting spell due to a lack of oxygen.

Doctor Lowe assured Kevin that the execution
would be painless, which it is, but I'm not sure he
heard.

Kevin's medical file indicated that he was a smoker
so I offered him a last cigarette. He kept laughing. I
told Kevin he had a minute to collect and compose
himself and offered him a chair. He fell on the chair
and continued laughing.

After the minute, I asked Kevin if he had any
last words or any last message he wished to have

transmitted. He did not seem to hear. I insisted, trying to make myself understood above the din of his cackling, but it was useless.

As I always do, and insist upon doing, I attempted to shake hands with Kevin to wish him, on my own personal behalf, farewell. But he hid his hand as if we were playing a game.

Mister Rothway and the guards conveyed Kevin to the gallows and made him stand straight over the trap. Mister Rothway tied his hands behind his back, covered his head with a hood and put the noose around his neck. To the very end, Kevin did not stop laughing.

At 7 a.m., the trap was released and your son Kevin died painlessly.

Please believe that I share in your grief.

Yours truly,

Harry Parlington
Director,
Cantos Correctional Institution

HP:ym

Manner
of
Dying 34

Dear Mrs. Barlow,

As director of Cantos Correctional Institution and
pursuant to the Right-to-Information law, I am writing
to inform you of how your son Kevin faced up to his
execution by hanging for the crimes he committed.

For his last supper, Kevin ordered: caviar; champagne; cigarillos. Though an unusual request, we
obliged. He gobbled down his caviar and drank his
champagne in seemingly a single gulp. He asked for
more champagne. I authorized another half-bottle.

When it disappeared equally quickly and he asked for a third, I refused. There are limits.

Kevin rudely did not avail himself of the services of Father Preston.

Periodic checks throughout the evening and night seemed to indicate that Kevin was agitated and did not sleep at all. He was seen smoking cigarillo after cigarillo, pacing about his cell and holding himself up to the window by his fingers to look out. At 10:11 p.m., I was informed that he was hollering for me. I could hear him a hundred yards away. He asked me why we were wasting his time and couldn't he be hanged right away. I ascribed this bravado to nervous tension and refused. I gave him another box of cigarillos.

At 6 a.m., when Father Preston's services were offered again, Kevin replied that he'd prefer a bartender and began to holler for me again.

When I arrived at 6:11 a.m., Kevin was kicking at the door of his cell, shouting for things to move. When the door was opened, he bounded out and had to be restrained by the guards, though with little violence, I assure you. I would describe your son as: angry and highly impatient. I began to read him the judgment concerning his execution as handed down by the legal and legitimate courts of the land in accordance with the law, but he kept interrupting with "Let's go! Let's go!" and had to be restrained again. I quickly finished, informed him that I was here to carry out this judgment and asked him if he understood this. Before I had even finished, he was shouting: "Yesyesyesyesyes!" I dispensed with asking him to accompany me.

In spite of the guards' efforts, we raced rather than walked down the corridor. When he caught sight of the gallows, Kevin charged for it so that he was half-way up the steps before Doctor Lowe could assure him that the execution would be painless, which it is. The guards brought him back down.

I offered Kevin a last cigarillo. He refused it. I told him he had a minute to collect and compose himself and offered him a chair. He refused angrily.

I did not insist and asked him if he had any last words or any last message he wished to have transmitted. He said: "Stop wasting my time!"

As I always do, and insist upon doing, I shook hands with Kevin and wished him, on my own personal behalf, farewell. He impatiently shook my hand and that of Doctor Lowe, Father Preston and Mister Rothway, wishing us all speedy promotions.

Kevin pushed and made another break for it and got to the top of the gallows before Mister Rothway or the guards. He put the noose around his neck and started kicking at the trap. Mister Rothway tied his hands behind his back, but did not bother with covering his head with a hood.

At 6:17 a.m., the trap was released and your son Kevin died painlessly.

Please believe that I share in your grief.

Yours truly,

Harry Parlington
Director,
Cantos Correctional Institution

HP:ym

Dear Mrs. Barlow,

As director of Cantos Correctional Institution and
pursuant to the Right-to-Information law, I am writing
to inform you of how your son Kevin faced up to his
execution by hanging for the crimes he committed.

For his last supper, Kevin ordered: a salad with a
blue-cheese dressing; two cheeseburgers (Cheddar
cheese) with the usual condiments; french fries; mineral
water; apple pie with vanilla ice-cream. He ate everything except for his hamburger patties, which he

wrapped in a napkin and left on his plate, and he asked for another bottle of mineral water.

Father Preston stayed with Kevin for one hour and twenty-two minutes. What transpired between them is protected by the code of ethics concerning professional secrets and is known only by Father Preston and the Almighty.

Periodic checks throughout the evening and night seemed to indicate that Kevin was very agitated and did not sleep at all. He was seen pacing about his cell frantically and holding himself up to the window by his fingers to look out.

At 6 a.m., when Father Preston's services were offered again, Kevin asked to see him. As the door was opened, Kevin made a fierce attempt to get away. Father Preston was hit in the face. The guards pushed Kevin back and closed the door. Kevin insisted that he wanted to confess. Father Preston was willing to go in again. The door was opened a second time and Kevin made a second attempt to get away. Once again he was rebuffed and the door was closed. Kevin still claimed that he wanted to see Father Preston. I was informed of what had happened. I deemed that Kevin was not acting in good faith and instructed that, if he wanted to speak with Father Preston, he would have to do so through the barred opening of the door. There are limits. Kevin and Father Preston spoke for four minutes. What transpired between them is protected by the code of ethics concerning professional secrets and is known only by Father Preston and the Almighty.

At 6:50 a.m., when I entered Kevin's cell with the attending personnel, we found that Kevin had attempted to block the door by jamming his blanket between it and the floor. Kevin was standing on the far side of the cell beneath the window, shouting at us to leave him alone. I would describe your son as: pale, frightened and extremely aggressive. In spite of his shouting, I read him the judgment concerning his execution as handed down by the legal and legitimate courts of the land in accordance with the law, informed him that I was here to carry out this judgment and asked him if he understood this. He shouted that he didn't. I repeated myself. When he still claimed not to understand, I deemed that he was not replying in good faith and asked him to accompany me. He refused. Unfortunately I must inform you that a very violent struggle ensued. I assure you, however, that only the force that was needed was used and no more.

As Kevin was carried down the corridor, he continued to struggle and to shout, doubling his efforts when he caught sight of the gallows.

Doctor Lowe assured Kevin that the execution would be painless, which it is, but I'm not sure he heard.

Kevin's medical file indicated that he was a smoker, but I dispensed with offering him a last cigarette. I told Kevin he had a minute to collect and compose himself and offered him a chair. He continued to struggle and the guards had to keep him on the floor to contain him.

After the minute, I asked Kevin if he had any last words or any last message he wished to have transmitted and I removed his gag. He spat at me.

As I always do, and insist upon doing, I attempted to shake hands with Kevin to wish him, on my own personal behalf, farewell. But his hands were tightly bound behind his back.

Mister Rothway and the guards carried Kevin to the gallows and held him over the trap. Mister Rothway forced a hood over Kevin's head and put the noose around his neck. To the very end, Kevin did not stop struggling and shouting.

At 7:04 a.m., the trap was released and your son Kevin died painlessly.

Please believe that I share in your grief.

Yours truly,

Harry Parlington
Director,
Cantos Correctional Institution

HP:ym

Manner
of
Dying 60

Dear Mrs. Barlow,

As director of Cantos Correctional Institution and
pursuant to the Right-to-Information law, I am writing
to inform you of how your son Kevin faced up to his
execution by hanging for the crimes he committed.

For his last supper, Kevin ordered: a pear. He did
not eat it.

Kevin did not avail himself of the services of Father
Preston and instead asked for pen and paper. He was
given a ballpoint pen and fifty sheets of lined paper.

Periodic checks throughout the evening and night seemed to indicate that Kevin was calm. He was seen pacing about his cell, and writing, sitting on the floor and using his bed as a desk. At 12:14 a.m., he asked for more paper. He was given an extra hundred sheets.

At 6 a.m., when Father Preston's services were offered again, Kevin once again refused.

At 6:50 a.m., when I entered Kevin's cell with the attending personnel, I found Kevin writing on his bed. I would describe your son as: pale, busy and flustered. Before I had even said a word, he pleaded that he be given a little more time, that he was nearly finished. To his left was an amazing pile of sheets of paper, each densely covered in handwriting, with here and there heavily scribbled-out mistakes. I asked Kevin how much more time he wanted. He replied: "Not long. Three more pages." In matters like this, I have a small amount of discretionary power. I told Kevin to call out when he was finished but to be quick. The door was closed and he was left in peace.

At 7:18 a.m., Kevin called out. When I entered his cell with the attending personnel, I found him holding himself up to the window by his fingers and looking out. The sheets of paper were neatly stacked on his bed. I would describe your son as: pale and calm. He thanked me for the extra time and asked me for a large envelope. I had one fetched. I read Kevin the judgment concerning his execution as handed down by the legal and legitimate courts of the land in accordance with the law, informed him that I was here to carry out this judgment and asked him if he understood this. Kevin said that he did. I asked him to accompany me. He walked out with me.

As we walked down the corridor, I slightly ahead of him and the others several feet behind, Kevin busied himself with putting the stack of papers in the large envelope and sealing it properly. When he caught sight of the gallows, Kevin became frightened, but he squeezed the envelope in his arms and this seemed to comfort him.

Doctor Lowe assured Kevin that the execution would be painless, which it is.

Kevin's medical file indicated that he was a smoker so I offered him a last cigarette. He declined it. I told Kevin he had a minute to collect and compose himself and offered him a chair. He sat down and attempted to write something on the front of the envelope, but his hand was trembling too much to hold the pen steadily. I knelt beside him and held the pen and his hand in my hand. We carefully wrote out your name and your address.

After the minute, I asked Kevin if he had any last words or any last message he wished to have trans-mitted. Slightly out of breath, he said: "Tell my mother here's her son and she mustn't be sad." And he handed me the envelope, which I enclose with this letter. I assured him that I would tell you and that you would receive the envelope.

As I always do, and insist on doing, I shook hands with Kevin and wished him, on my own personal behalf, farewell.

Kevin walked up to the gallows with Mister Rothway and stood over the trap. At this time, he said: "It *is* a beautiful world, isn't it?" I agreed with him that it was. Mister Rothway covered his head with a hood, tied his hands behind his back and put the noose around his neck.

At 7:29 a.m., the trap was released and your son Kevin died painlessly.

Please believe that I share in your grief.

Yours truly,

Harry Parlington
Director,
Cantos Correctional Institution

enc.
HP:ym

Manner
of
Dying 85

Dear Mrs. Barlow,

As director of Cantos Correctional Institution and
pursuant to the Right-to-Information law, I am writing
to inform you of how your son Kevin faced up to his
execution by hanging for the crimes he committed.

For his last supper, Kevin ordered: two grilled hot
dogs with the usual condiments; french fries; root beer.
He ate everything except for his hot-dog wieners, which
he wrapped in a napkin and left on his plate, and he
asked for another bottle of root beer.

Father Preston stayed with Kevin for fifty-five minutes. What transpired between them is protected by the code of ethics concerning professional secrets and is known only by Father Preston and the Almighty.

Periodic checks throughout the evening and night seemed to indicate that Kevin was agitated and did not sleep at all. He was seen pacing about his cell and holding himself up to the window by his fingers to look out. At 2:36 a.m., I was informed that Kevin wanted to see me. He asked me if he could go outside. In matters like this, I have a small amount of discretionary power. Cantos has a large, secure interior courtyard. I instructed the guards to escort Kevin to it and to keep a good eye on him but otherwise to let him do as he pleased. Kevin spent the whole night stretching; doing push-ups, sit-ups and other calisthenics; walking in circles; running on the spot; shadow-boxing; lying on the ground looking up at the sky. It was a cool clear night. One could see one's breath and countless stars.

At 6 a.m., when Father Preston's services were offered again, Kevin asked to see him. What transpired between them is protected by the code of ethics concerning professional secrets and is known only by Father Preston and the Almighty.

At 6:50 a.m., when I entered the courtyard with the attending personnel, I found Kevin and Father Preston slowly walking in circles. I would describe your son as: pale, flushed and nervous. I read him the judgment concerning his execution as handed down by the legal and legitimate courts of the land in accordance with the law, informed him that I was here to carry out this judgment and asked him if he understood this. Kevin nodded. I asked him to accompany me. He followed me.

As we walked down the corridor, I slightly ahead of him and the others several feet behind, Kevin shadow-boxed. When he caught sight of the gallows, Kevin went into a frenzy of jabbing, uppercutting and head-dodging.

Doctor Lowe assured Kevin that the execution would be painless, which it is. Kevin nodded.

Kevin's medical file indicated that he was a smoker so I offered him a last cigarette. He shook his head. I told Kevin he had a minute to collect and compose himself and offered him a chair. He nodded but stayed on his feet and continued to shadow-box.

After the minute, I asked Kevin if he had any last words or any last message he wished to have trans-mitted. He said: "I'll win. Knockout."

As I always do, and insist upon doing, I shook hands with Kevin and wished him, on my own personal behalf, farewell.

Kevin slowly jogged up to the gallows with Mister Rothway and the guards and stood over the trap. Mister Rothway tied his hands behind his back, covered his head with a hood and put the noose around his neck. Kevin jogged on the spot and began to hyperventilate loudly.

At 7 a.m., the trap was released and your son Kevin died painlessly.

Please believe that I share in your grief.

Yours truly,

Harry Parlington
Director,
Cantos Correctional Institution

HP:ym

Dear Mrs. Barlow,

As director of Cantos Correctional Institution and pursuant to the Right-to-Information law, I am writing to inform you of how your son Kevin faced up to his execution by hanging for the crimes he committed.

For his last supper, Kevin ordered: a T-bone steak; green beans and potatoes; beer; pistachio ice-cream. He did not touch any of it except for the ice-cream.

Kevin did not avail himself of the services of Father Preston.

Periodic checks throughout the evening and night seemed to indicate that Kevin was agitated and did not sleep at all. He was seen pacing about his cell and holding himself up to the window by his fingers to look out. At 10:24 p.m., he asked for some magazines. He was given a wide range of political, sports and general-interest magazines. At 10:47 p.m., I was informed that Kevin wanted to see me. He asked me if I wanted to play backgammon. I don't like games of chance — I find chance disturbing — but I agreed. I sent a guard to fetch a game. Kevin and I played backgammon all night. We also talked, he to me for the most part. I asked him if he wanted to have our conversation taped as a final gift to you. He agreed. A tape recorder was brought into the cell. I enclose the four tapes with this letter. Kevin beat me handily.

At 6 a.m., when Father Preston's services were offered again, Kevin once again refused. I asked him if he wanted to stop playing. He wanted to continue. But he did not play as well as before.

At 6:52 a.m., upon finishing a game, I told Kevin that it was time. He nodded. I would describe your son as: pale and frightened. The door of the cell was opened and the attending personnel entered. I read Kevin the judgment concerning his execution as handed down by the legal and legitimate courts of the land in accordance with the law, informed him that I was here to carry out this judgment and asked him if he understood this. He nodded. I asked him to accompany me. Clutching the backgammon board, Kevin stood up and walked out with me. One of the guards attempted to retrieve the board, but Kevin shouted and I told the guard to let him keep it.

As we walked down the corridor, Kevin had difficulty staying on his feet and required the assistance of the guards. When he caught sight of the gallows, Kevin relieved himself in his pants.

Doctor Lowe assured Kevin that the execution would be painless, which it is.

Kevin's medical file indicated that he was a smoker so I offered him a last cigarette. He did not respond. I told Kevin he had a minute to collect and compose himself and offered him a chair. He sat down. At this time, out of breath and with great difficulty of articulation, he said: "I'm really sorry about all this." I replied that I was too.

After the minute, I asked Kevin if he had any last words or any last message he wished to have transmitted. He repeated: "I'm really sorry about all this." Again I replied that I was too.

As I always do, and insist upon doing, I attempted to shake hands with Kevin to wish him, on my own personal behalf, farewell. But he would not let go of the backgammon board.

Kevin seemed unable to support himself so Mister Rothway and the guards conveyed him to the gallows and helped him stand over the trap. Mister Rothway covered his head with a hood and put the noose around his neck, but did not bother with tying his hands behind his back. In the last seconds, Kevin was holding on to the backgammon board so tightly that it cracked loudly into several pieces.

At 7:01 a.m., the trap was released and your son Kevin died painlessly.

Please believe that I share in your grief.

Yours truly,

Harry Parlington
Director,
Cantos Correctional Institution

enc.
HP:ym

Manner
of
Dying 96

Dear Mrs. Barlow,

As director of Cantos Correctional Institution and
pursuant to the Right-to-Information law, I am
writing to inform you of how your son Kevin faced
up to his execution by hanging for the crimes he
committed.

For his last supper, Kevin did not order anything. I
came round to tell him that he could have practically
anything he wanted, but he said that he was not
hungry. I told him that if he changed his mind and

wanted something to eat, he should ask the guards, no matter the hour.

Father Preston stayed with Kevin all evening and all night. What transpired between them is protected by the code of ethics concerning professional secrets and is known only by Father Preston and the Almighty.

Periodic checks throughout the evening and night seemed to indicate that Kevin was very agitated and did not sleep at all. He was seen pacing about his cell, sitting on his bed, holding himself up to the window by his fingers to look out, and kneeling on the floor with his head on Father Preston's lap. Frequently throughout the night he was heard sobbing.

At 6:50 a.m., when I entered Kevin's cell with the attending personnel, I found Father Preston sitting on the bed and Kevin sitting on the floor in the far corner of the cell beneath the window. I would describe your son as: pale, puffy-faced and very frightened. I read him the judgment concerning his execution as handed down by the legal and legitimate courts of the land in accordance with the law, informed him that I was here to carry out this judgment and asked him if he understood this. Kevin began to weep. I believe he understood me and I asked him to accompany me. He did not move. As soon as the guards touched him, Kevin began to sob loudly and to beg for mercy. He begged repeatedly. I explained to him that unfortunately it was beyond my power to do anything. The guards lifted Kevin to his feet and carried him out. I assure you there was no violence.

As Kevin was conveyed down the corridor, he continued to sob and to beg. When he caught sight of the gallows, Kevin relieved himself in his pants and began to thrash about. Suddenly he clutched his left shoulder, whimpered, "I'm not feeling well," and collapsed. Doctor Lowe was there instantly, but in spite of several minutes of vigorous cardiopulmonary resuscitation, he could not get the heart going again, and, at 7:06 a.m., had to acknowledge Kevin's death. I remember that while his body was motionless and getting cold, his eyes were still on me.

This is not the way I would have had it. None of this is the way I would have had it.

Please believe that I share in your grief.

Yours truly,

Harry Parlington
Director,
Cantos Correctional Institution

HP:ym

The Mirror Machine

I remember how I met
my husband. My dear
sweet husband. I was
sixteen and I was
dressed in white. I was
also wearing a straw hat
only it was too small
and I was always losing
it in the wind. This was
in Grande-Rivière. I
was staying with Father

Bouillon for a few
weeks during the
summer. I was standing
on the veranda,
considering whether I
should go for a walk
with this too-small hat
and always have to keep
my hand on my head to
hold it down or
whether I should fetch
another hat that fit me
perfectly but didn't go
as well with my dress. I
was standing on the
veranda, thinking about
it, when a car with two
men drove up and
stalled just in front of
the house, maybe fifty
feet away. The driver
came out. I knew he
was a doctor because
his car had the special
licence plate that
doctors had at the time.
He opened the hood on
the side of the car
opposite me, leaned in

and did I don't know
what. He seemed in a
hurry. The other man
didn't help; he just sat
in the car, listless. I
found out later my
husband was driving
him to the hospital. He
fiddled about with the
engine for a minute or
two and then fetched
the crank. He turned
the crank and the
engine started up with
a roar. He hurried back
into the car. I watched
this scene without
moving or saying a
word. He didn't see me,
the doctor. The other
man did. The car
disappeared down the
road and then the wind
blew my hat away. I
went for a long walk,
my hand on my head to
hold my hat on. I will
never blah-blah-blah-
blah-blah-blah-blah-

Heavens, she can go on.

blah-blah-blah-blah-
blah-blah-blah-blah-
blah-blah-blah-blah-
blah-blah-blah-blah-
blah-blah-blah-blah-
blah-blah-blah-blah-
blah-blah-blah-blah-
blah-blah-blah-blah-
blah-blah-blah-blah-
blah-blah-blah-blah-
blah-blah-blah-blah-
blah-blah-blah-blah-
blah-blah-blah-blah-
blah-blah-blah-blah-
blah-blah-blah-blah-
blah-blah-blah-blah-
blah-blah-blah-blah-
blah-blah-blah-blah-
blah-blah-blah-blah-
blah-blah-blah-blah-
blah-blah-blah-blah-
blah-blah-blah-blah-
blah-blah-blah-blah-
blah-blah-blah-blah-
blah-blah-blah-blah-
blah-blah-blah-blah-
blah-blah-blah-blah-
blah-blah-blah-blah-

blah-blah-blah-blah-
blah-blah-blah-blah-
blah-blah-blah-blah-
blah-blah-blah-blah-
blah-blah-blah-blah-
blah-blah-blah-blah-
blah-blah-blah-blah-
blah-blah-blah-blah-
blah-blah-blah-blah-
blah-blah-blah-blah-
blah-blah-blah-blah-
blah-blah-blah-blah-
blah-blah-blah-blah-
blah-blah-blah-blah-
blah-blah-blah-blah-
blah-blah-blah-blah-
blah-blah-blah-blah-
blah-blah-blah-blah-
blah-blah-blah-blah-
blah-blah-blah-blah-
blah-blah-blah-blah-
blah-blah-blah-blah-
blah-blah-blah-blah-
blah-blah-blah-blah-
blah-blah-blah-blah-
blah-blah-blah-blah-
blah-blah-blah-blah-
blah-blah-blah-blah-
blah-blah-blah-blah-

blah-blah-blah-blah-
blah-blah-blah-blah-
blah-blah-blah-blah-
blah-blah-blah-blah-
blah-blah-blah-blah-
blah-blah-blah-blah-
blah-blah-blah-blah-
blah-blah-blah-blah-
blah-blah-blah-blah-
blah-blah-blah-blah-
blah-blah-blah-blah-
blah-blah-blah-blah-
blah-blah-blah-blah-
blah-blah-blah-blah-
blah-blah-blah-blah-
blah-blah-blah-blah-
blah-blah-blah-blah-
blah-blah-blah-blah-
blah-blah-blah-blah-
blah-blah-blah-blah-
blah-blah-blah-blah-
blah-blah-blah-blah-
blah-blah-blah-blah-
blah-blah-blah-blah-
blah-blah-blah-blah-
blah-blah-blah-blah-
blah-blah-blah-blah-

blah-blah-blah-blah-
blah-blah-blah-blah-
blah-blah-blah-blah-
blah-blah-blah-blah-
blah-blah-blah-blah-
blah-blah-blah-blah-
blah-blah-blah-blah-
blah-blah-blah-blah-
blah-blah-blah-blah-
blah-blah-blah-blah-
blah-blah-blah-blah-
blah-blah-blah-blah-   My head will explode soon.
blah-blah-blah-blah-
blah-blah-blah-blah-
blah-blah-blah-blah-
blah-blah-blah-blah-
blah-blah-blah-blah-
blah-blah-blah-blah-
blah-blah-blah-blah-
blah-blah-blah-blah-
blah-blah-blah-blah-
blah-blah-blah-blah-
blah-blah-blah-blah-
blah-blah-blah-blah-
blah-blah-blah-blah-
blah-blah-blah-blah-
blah-blah-blah-blah-
blah-blah-blah-blah-
blah-blah-blah-blah-

blah-blah-blah-blah-
blah-blah-blah-blah-
blah-blah-blah-blah-
blah-blah-blah-blah-
blah-blah-blah-blah-
blah-blah-blah-blah-

(Meanwhile, the machine was chugging away industriously. I put my hand on it. I could feel vibrations.)

blah-blah-blah-blah-
blah-blah-blah-blah-
blah-blah-blah-blah-
blah-blah-blah-blah-
blah-blah-blah-blah-
blah-blah-blah-blah-
blah-blah-blah-blah-
blah-blah-blah-blah-
blah-blah-blah-blah-
blah-blah-blah-blah-
next day, a bright sunny
day, I was walking back
home from the post
office when I saw the
very same car coming
towards me. The sun
was behind me, in the
doctor's eyes. His car

didn't have visors so he was wearing a long cap. As the car came closer I could see something was written on this cap. "SEARCHING FOR A BRIDE" it said, in bright red letters. He was a bachelor of course. He told me later this cap was a gift from a friend. And so, squinting at the road ahead, as if actually searching for a bride at that very moment, he drove by. Without seeing me, once again. He was so charmingly distracted sometimes. Once he blah-blah-blah-blah-blah-blah-blah-blah-blah-blah-blah-blah-blah-blah-blah-blah-blah-blah-blah-blah-blah-blah-blah-blah-blah-blah-blah-blah-blah-blah-blah-blah-blah-blah-blah-blah-

blah-blah-blah-blah-
blah-blah-blah-blah-
blah-blah-blah-blah-
blah-blah-blah-blah-
blah-blah-blah-blah-
blah-blah-blah-blah-
blah-blah-blah-blah-

*(I was visiting my grandmother and I had found this
machine in her basement. It looked at first like nothing
more than a wooden box.)*

blah-blah-blah-blah-
blah-blah-blah-blah-
blah-blah-blah-blah-
blah-blah-blah-blah-
blah-blah-blah-blah-
blah-blah-blah-blah-
blah-blah-blah-blah-
blah-blah-blah-blah-
blah-blah-blah-blah-
blah-blah-blah-blah-
blah-blah-blah-blah-
blah-blah-blah-blah-
blah-blah-blah-blah-
blah-blah-blah-blah-
blah-blah-blah-blah-
blah-blah-blah-blah-

blah-blah-blah-blah-
blah-blah-blah-blah-
blah-blah-blah-blah-
blah-blah-blah-blah-
blah-blah-blah-blah-
blah-blah-blah-blah-
blah-blah-blah-blah-
blah-blah-blah-blah-
blah-blah-blah-blah-
blah-blah-blah-blah-
blah-blah-blah-blah-
blah-blah-blah-blah-
blah-blah-blah-blah-
blah-blah-blah-blah-
blah-blah-blah-blah-
blah-blah-blah-blah-

(More junk, more debris, I thought.)

blah-blah-blah-blah-
blah-blah-blah-blah-
blah-blah-blah-blah-
blah-blah-blah-blah-
blah-blah-blah-blah-
blah-blah-blah-blah-
blah-blah-blah-blah-
blah-blah-blah-blah-
blah-blah-blah-blah-
blah-blah-blah-blah-

blah-blah-blah-blah-

(My grandmother, you see, clings to her possessions. She throws away nothing. Everything has value. As a young wife she suffered through the Depression, and shortly after the war her husband died, leaving her alone to raise four children. She suffered through loss, loneliness, poverty, tough times. By dint of hard work, multiple jobs, careful investments and frugality, she managed to raise her children— with great success, in fact: she produced a cloistered Benedictine nun, a doctor, a diplomat poet and a well-known journalist—but like anyone who has had to struggle hard, she can't forget the price of every success along her difficult road. Having known the word "want" for too long, she cannot understand its antonym, "enough". I sometimes think she's like that gold prospector in the Jack London tale who, months after being rescued from starvation, still hoards nuts, biscuits, tinned food and dried fish in his pockets and in every nook and cranny of his room.)

blah-blah-blah-blah-
blah-blah-blah-blah-
blah-blah-blah-blah-
blah-blah-blah-blah-
blah-blah-blah-blah-
blah-blah-blah-blah-
blah-blah-blah-blah-
blah-blah-blah-blah-
blah-blah-blah-blah-

blah-blah-blah-blah-
blah-blah-blah-blah-
blah-blah-blah-blah-
blah-blah-blah-blah-
blah-blah-blah-blah-
blah-blah-blah-blah-
blah-blah-blah-blah-
blah-blah-blah-blah-
blah-blah-blah-blah-

(I made to push the box aside. It wasn't what I was looking for. I was looking for my grandmother's snowshoe moccasins. I was on all fours, buried in the cold closet where she keeps her coats. She had it in mind that we would go snowshoeing (even though there was only one pair of snowshoes, but no matter, I was young, she said, I would follow along, sinking three feet into the snow at every step). But the box was unexpectedly heavy, a good fifteen pounds. I was curious, so I pulled it out. What icon was this?)

blah-blah-blah-blah-
blah-blah-blah-blah-
blah-blah-blah-blah-
blah-blah-blah-blah-
blah-blah-blah-blah-
blah-blah-blah-blah-
blah-blah-blah-blah-
blah-blah-blah-blah-
blah-blah-blah-blah-

blah-blah-blah-blah-
blah-blah-blah-blah-
blah-blah-blah-blah-
blah-blah-blah-blah-
blah-blah-blah-blah-
blah-blah-blah-blah-

(My grandmother, you see, is a late twentieth-century ani-mist. Every object in her house is infused with a conscious life, with an indwelling psyche, that speaks to her of some-body or something from her long life. She lives alone in this village on the south shore of the St. Lawrence, but sometimes her small house feels like a bustling metropolis of spirits.)

blah-blah-blah-blah-
blah-blah-blah-blah-
blah-blah-blah-blah-
blah-blah-blah-blah-
blah-blah carrying a
tray with cups and
cookies. And who
should I see standing
squarely in the living
room—I can still see
him perfectly! Standing
so straight. Looking out
with his kind face and
beautiful eyes. It was
Doctor "Searching for a

Bride". He smiled at
me and I at him,
though bashfully, I was
only sixteen you
understand. Father
Bouillon had invited
the new doctor in
town, telling him his
house would be full of
pretty girls. We spoke
to each other a little
that day and some more
in the next two weeks
each time he came by.
He was so earnest and
attentive to my every
word. Later he told me
that on that very first
day, as he was leaving,
he whispered to Father
Bouillon, "There's my
wife." I thought he was
very blah-blah-blah-
blah-blah-blah-blah-
blah-blah-blah-blah-
blah-blah-blah-blah-
blah-blah-blah-blah-
blah-blah-blah-blah-
blah-blah-blah-blah-

blah-blah-blah-blah-
blah-blah-blah-blah-

*(And evidently this machine was yet another resident goblin.
It was made of nicely burnished walnut and was about fifteen inches long, twelve inches wide and eight inches high. It
was some sort of mechanical device. A half-inch slit ran the
length of one of the long sides, right near the bottom. It had
lips of red velvet which revealed, when pulled back, a series
of ten or so rollers. Clearly, some thing, some product, came
in or out this way. On the side of the box opposite this slit
were two things: a thermometer-like tube embedded into the
wood with two gradations marked in red, MAX near the top
and MIN near the bottom; and a tiny horizontal door with
a round doorknob. The words "HIGH-GRADE WHITE
SAND ONLY" were inscribed on this door and it opened
with a click. There were rounded panels on each side. On
one of these I could read the sentence "DO NOT FILL OVER
THIS LINE". I put my finger down into the opening, but I
could only feel the inside walls of a cavity. I couldn't reach
the bottom. There were three holes on the top of the machine:
a small one near the edge, level with the thermometer-like
tube, with the words "HIGH-GRADE LIQUID SILVER
ONLY" inscribed around it; another in the opposite corner,
this one surrounded by the words "HIGH-GRADE OIL
ONLY" (this was obviously a high-grade machine); and,
finally, a third, larger, cork-stopped hole midway along one
of the widths. In the centre was the only clue as to the
machine's function: a clean, oblong plaque neatly affixed*

with golden nails. "THE VITA ETERNA MIRROR COM-
PANY, PORT HOPE, ONTARIO", it said. "MIRRORS TO
LAST TILL KINGDOM COME".)

blah-blah-blah-blah-
blah-blah-blah-blah-
blah-blah-blah-blah-
blah-blah-blah-blah-
blah-blah-blah-blah-
blah-blah-blah-blah-
blah-blah-blah-blah-
blah-blah-blah-blah-
blah-blah-blah-blah-
blah-blah-blah-blah-
blah-blah-blah-blah-
blah-blah-blah-blah-
blah-blah-blah-blah-
blah-blah-blah-blah-
blah-blah-blah-blah-
blah-blah-blah-blah-
blah-blah-blah-blah-
blah-blah-blah-blah-
blah-blah-blah-blah-

("Have you found them? Must I come down?" came a voice
from above, vacillating on the edge between annoyance and
enquiry.
*   "Not yet. A minute more." I penetrated the closet again.*

Among quantities of shoes, boots, slippers and sneakers, I found moccasins. And near where the machine had been I came upon a grey felt bag with the Vita Eterna Mirror Company imprint on it. I brought it out. Replacing disturbed footwear and displaced coathangers with the care of an archaeologist, I closed the closet door, gathered up the results of my dig and made my way upstairs from the basement.)

blah-blah-blah-blah-
blah-blah-blah-blah-
blah-blah-blah-blah-
blah-blah-blah-blah-
blah-blah-blah-blah-
blah-blah-blah-blah-
blah-blah-blah-blah-
blah-blah-blah-blah-
blah-blah-blah-blah-
blah-blah-blah-blah-
blah-blah-blah-blah-
blah-blah-blah-blah-
blah-blah-blah-blah-
blah-blah-blah-blah-
blah-blah-blah-blah-
blah-blah-blah-blah-
blah-blah-blah-blah-
blah-blah-blah-blah-
blah-blah-blah-blah-
blah-blah-blah-blah-

blah-blah-blah-blah-
blah-blah-blah-blah-
blah-blah-blah-blah-
blah-blah-blah-blah-
blah-blah-blah-blah-
blah-blah-blah-blah-
blah-blah-blah-blah-

(She was at the top of the stairs. She is a woman in her early eighties. She is vain in a dignified way and dresses well, invariably in one shade or another of purple, her favourite colour. Except for a few of the normal indignities of old age—cataracts (operated on), a little arthritis, a certain physical sagging—she is in perfect health. Because she saves up all the conversation that she can't have when she's alone and lonely, she talks nonstop. She listens, but sometimes not really; sometimes one's words are like a table of contents from which she'll choose a word or phrase that will set her off. Her beliefs are solid and well constructed, nearly impregnable, and her ways, though not intolerant, are nonetheless fixed. Great Questions do not disturb her any more; her questions now are well within the limits of the Great Answers that have brought her comfort all her life. She loves me, for sure, but with the bias of her age. My lack of religiousness (she can't bring herself to use the correct words: fulminating atheist) saddens her, and my existential hesitations (as exemplified by the fact that I'm nearer to thirty than to twenty yet have still never held down a real, steady job, have accomplished precious little in my life) my hesitations make her

impatient because she can't understand them. She thinks I'm lost. We are meant to stand firm like a house, she tells me, not to be tossed about like a ship. To her the world, the universe, is an orderly place run by God where goodness and hard work are ultimately rewarded and evil and sloth ultimately punished. She is a poor loser at cards—worse than me—and she cheats outrageously. My grandmother loves me and I love my grandmother—which doesn't mean that we always get along.)

blah-blah-blah-blah-
blah-blah-blah-blah-
blah-blah-blah-blah-
blah-blah-blah-blah-
blah-blah-blah-blah-
blah-blah-blah-blah-
blah-blah-blah-blah-
blah-blah-blah-blah-
blah-blah-blah-blah-
blah-blah-blah-blah-
blah-blah-blah-blah-
blah-blah-blah-blah-
blah-blah-blah-blah-
blah-blah-blah-blah-
blah-blah-blah-blah-
blah-blah-blah-blah-
blah-blah-blah-blah-
blah-blah-blah-blah-

blah-blah-blah-blah-
blah-blah-blah-blah-
blah-blah-blah-blah-
blah-blah-blah-blah-
blah-blah-blah-blah-

("What's this?" she asked.

"That was my question," I replied.

"Oh my," she exclaimed when she took a closer look. Her voice changed. "That old thing. I'd forgotten we still had it." She ran her fingers along it.)

blah-blah-blah-blah-
blah-blah-blah-blah-
blah-blah-blah-blah-
blah-blah-blah-blah-
blah-blah-blah-blah-
blah-blah-blah-blah-
blah-blah-blah-blah-
blah-blah-blah-blah-
blah-blah-blah-blah-
blah-blah-blah-blah-
blah-blah-blah-blah-
blah-blah-blah-blah-
blah-blah-blah-blah-
blah-blah-blah-blah-
blah-blah-blah-blah-
blah-blah-blah-blah-
blah-blah-blah-blah-

blah-blah-blah-blah-
blah-blah-blah-blah-
blah-blah-blah-blah-
blah-blah-blah-blah-
blah-blah-blah-blah-
blah-blah-blah-blah-
blah-blah-blah-blah-
blah-blah-blah-blah-
blah-blah-blah-blah-
blah-blah-blah-blah-

(I looked about her lair. I will just mention that my grand-mother's house is cluttered with furniture that clashes in style; that she owns no complete set of cutlery or dishware or kitchenware or glassware or bedsheets or towels, but only the accumulated veterans of six decades of housekeeping. I will not mention the religious paraphernalia (the large crucifix over the front door, the lithographs of the Virgin and her brood, the tourist-shop foreign icons, the hanging rosary, the Pope's colour photos, etc.) nor the fact that after her children left her she embarked on organized world travels and brought back home the bric-à-brac of the Indies (an ouzo-bottle lamp, pseudo-antique Greek vases, Easter Island-like sculptures, African masks, a Swiss cuckoo clock, a huge Pacific shell, a Tunisian birdcage, purple Russian babushka dolls, Chinese china, etc.) nor the fact that she likes fishing and gardening (she's well equipped, believe me)—there's much that I leave out. Cubic metres. A bloated etcetera of goods, chattels and knick-knacks. My grandmother has a

sort of Midas touch: every object she touches becomes eternal.
And did I mention that her house is tiny? That there's no real
division between her living room, her dining room, her
kitchen and the piano?)

blah-blah-blah-blah-
blah-blah-blah-blah-
blah-blah-blah-blah-
blah-blah-blah-blah-
blah-blah-blah-blah-
blah-blah-blah-blah-
blah-blah-blah-blah-
blah-blah-blah-blah-
blah-blah-blah-blah-
blah-blah-blah-blah-
blah-blah-blah-blah-
blah-blah-blah-blah-
blah-blah-blah-blah-

(I brought the machine to the kitchen table and set the moc-
casins on the floor.
 "So what is it?" I asked.
 "It's an old appliance. It's a mirror machine."
 As she said this, she nodded towards the living room, at
the large mirror above the fireplace. I looked at it.)

blah-blah-blah-blah-
blah-blah-blah-blah-
blah-blah-blah-blah-

blah-blah-blah-blah-
blah-blah-blah-blah-
blah-blah-blah-blah-
blah-blah-blah-blah-
blah-blah-blah-blah-
blah-blah-blah-blah-
blah-blah-blah-blah-
blah-blah-blah-blah-
blah-blah-blah-blah-
blah-blah-blah-blah-
blah-blah-blah-blah-
blah-blah-blah-blah-
blah-blah-blah-blah-
blah-blah-blah-blah-
blah-blah-blah-blah-

(In the reflected rectangle I could see the rounded shoulders and white mane of an old woman and the serious expression of a young man.)

blah-blah-blah-blah-
blah-blah-blah-blah-
blah-blah-blah-blah-
blah-blah-blah-blah-
blah-blah-blah-blah-
blah-blah-blah-blah-
blah-blah-blah-blah-
blah-blah-blah-blah-

blah-blah-blah-blah-
blah-blah-blah-blah-
blah-blah-blah-blah-
blah-blah-blah-blah-

("What do you mean by a mirror machine?"

"It's a machine that makes mirrors. This is how we used to make mirrors when I was a girl."

I had never heard of such a thing. "Does it still work?"

"I think so. I don't see why not. Let's see...."

She sat down and with her twisted, impatient fingers she opened the felt bag. I sat down beside her. She pulled out a grey plastic bottle. "LIQUID SILVER" it said, in silver letters. She twisted the cap, turned the bottle upside down and placed the nozzle into the silver hole atop the machine. But as she squeezed the bottle, the nozzle jumped and a heavy, round drop formed on the wood.)

blah-blah-blah-blah-
blah-blah-blah-blah-
blah-blah-blah-blah-
blah-blah-blah-blah-
blah-blah-blah-blah-
blah-blah-blah-blah-
blah-blah-blah-blah-
blah-blah-blah-blah-
blah-blah-blah-blah-
blah-blah-blah-blah-
blah-blah-blah-blah-

blah-blah-blah-blah-

(*"Here, I'll do it,"* I said.

The bottle, for its size, was remarkably heavy. I looked closely at the drop of silver. I teased its tense surface with the nozzle. I squeezed the bottle, increasing the size of the drop, and then let go, sucking it in.)

blah-blah-blah-blah-
blah-blah-blah-blah-
blah-blah-blah-blah-
blah-blah-blah-blah-
blah-blah-blah-blah-
blah-blah-blah-blah-
blah-blah-blah-blah-
blah-blah-blah-blah-
blah-blah-blah-blah-
blah-blah-blah-blah-
blah-blah-blah-blah-
blah-blah-blah-blah-

(*"Good,"* said my grandmother. *"Silver is expensive."*)

blah-blah-blah-blah-
blah-blah-blah-blah-
blah-blah-blah-blah-
blah-blah-blah-blah-
blah-blah-blah-blah-
blah-blah-blah-blah-

blah-blah-blah-blah-
blah-blah-blah-blah-
blah-blah-blah-blah-

(I fitted the nozzle into the hole and squeezed. A column of silver appeared at the bottom of the tube. I let it rise. When it was half-way between the MIN and MAX marks, my grandmother said, "That's enough." I squeezed a second longer and stopped.)

blah-blah-blah-blah-
blah-blah-blah-blah-
blah-blah-blah-blah-
blah-blah-blah-blah-
blah-blah-blah-blah-
blah-blah-blah-blah-
blah-blah-blah-blah-
blah-blah-blah-blah-
blah-blah-blah-blah-
blah-blah-blah-blah-
blah-blah-blah-blah-
blah-blah-blah-blah-

(Next she brought out sand and a small oil bottle. The sand was in a cardboard carton. It was black, yellow and white and had an elaborate yet awkward drawing of a black man standing on a beach. He had a wide, colonized-and-happy-about-it grin and wore a straw hat that seemed to be rapidly unthatching and clothes that were very

studied in the way they were tattered, with shirt and pant cuffs that were precisely jagged. "NOVAK'S FINE WHITE" announced the sky above him. In smaller, ornate letters around some indecipherable coat of arms I could read "Purveyors of Fine White Sand to His Majesty's Household".)

blah-blah-blah-blah-
blah-blah-blah-blah-
blah-blah-blah-blah-
blah-blah-blah-blah-
blah-blah-blah-blah-
blah-blah-blah-blah-
blah-blah-blah-blah-
blah-blah-blah-blah-

("Some people would use cheap sand, sand they'd find around here," said my grandmother. "But it makes for smoky mirrors. The best sand comes from the Caribbean.")

blah-blah-blah-blah-
blah-blah-blah-blah-
blah-blah-blah-blah-
blah-blah-blah-blah-
blah-blah-blah-blah-
blah-blah-blah-blah-
blah-blah-blah-blah-
blah-blah-blah-blah-
blah-blah-blah-blah-

blah-blah-blah-blah-
blah-blah-blah-blah-

(While she poured sand through the door, I squirted oil into the machine.)

blah-blah-blah-blah-
blah-blah-blah-blah-
blah-blah-blah-blah-
blah-blah-blah-blah-
blah-blah-blah-blah-
blah-blah-blah-blah-
blah-blah-blah-blah-

(My grandmother sighed. "It must be fifty years since I last used this machine. Even in my time it was old and out of fashion. Now it's so much easier. You just go to a hardware store and you can buy an industrially manufactured, clear mirror any size or shape you want."

She paused. She was staring into midair. Her lips trembled.

"Ohhhhh, your grandfather used to rage at this machine, rage. *He who was normally such a patient man. He would jump up and want to rush out and buy a mirror that very minute. 'But we can't afford it!' I would tell him. 'We don't have the money. And the machine was given to us. We might as well use it.' He would fume. But we* really *didn't have the money. What do you expect? He wasn't a money man. He would treat his patients for nothing, would even buy them*

*the medicine he prescribed. 'Go—go for a walk—go rest—
go read, I'll finish,' I'd tell him. 'Away you go!' But he would
just look at me with his oh so beautiful eyes. Then he'd sit
down beside me again and we would finish together."*

She sighed tremulously.

*"The long patient hours we spent on this machine. I can't
count them, I cannot count them." She swallowed. Her eyes
were red.)*

blah-blah-blah-blah-
blah-blah-blah-blah-
blah-blah-blah-blah-
blah-blah-blah-blah-
blah-blah-blah-blah-
blah-blah-blah-blah-
blah-blah-blah-blah-
blah-blah-blah-blah-
blah-blah-blah-blah-
blah-blah-blah-blah-
blah-blah-blah-blah-
blah-blah-blah-blah-
blah-blah-blah-blah-
blah-blah-blah-blah-
blah-blah-blah-blah-
blah-blah-blah-blah-
blah-blah-blah-blah-
blah-blah-blah-blah-
blah-blah-blah-blah-

blah-blah-blah-blah-
blah-blah-blah-blah-
blah-blah-blah-blah-
blah-blah-blah-blah-

(On any other day I would have jostled her souvenirs aside and bluntly asked her how this contraption worked, but that day, for no particular reason, I let her come round in her slow, anecdotal way. I eyed the fireplace. I had noticed that her mirrors weren't perfect. They all had ridges that distorted the reflection, and various stains and marks. But I had ascribed these defects to age, not to handicraft origin.)

blah-blah-blah-blah-
blah-blah-blah-blah-
blah-blah-blah-blah-
blah-blah-blah-blah-
blah-blah-blah-blah-
blah-blah-blah-blah-
blah-blah-blah-blah-
blah-blah-blah-blah-
blah-blah-blah-blah-
blah-blah-blah-blah-
blah-blah-blah-blah-
blah-blah-blah-blah-
blah-blah-blah-blah-

(She rubbed her face with her hands. She looked at the

machine. "I wonder if it still works," she said quietly.)

blah-blah-blah-blah-
blah-blah-blah-blah-
blah-blah-blah-blah-
blah-blah-blah-blah-
blah-blah-blah-blah-
blah-blah-blah-blah-
blah-blah-blah-blah-

(She extracted from the bag the most amazing thing. It looked like a fossil. It was a horn. Like for a gramophone, only smaller. The narrow end joined into a short, shiny brass tube with screw threads. The other end curved and flared out, with the edges looking like the petals of a flower. My instinct was to think it was made of plastic, but it was genuine, politically incorrect ivory. Creamy white and cool and streaked with very fine black veins. It had intricate arabesque decorations on the outside, and lines that spiralled downwards on the inside. My grandmother pulled the cork from the third hole atop the machine and screwed in the horn. It could be rotated 360 degrees.)

blah-blah-blah-blah-
blah-blah-blah-blah-
blah-blah-blah-blah-
blah-blah-blah-blah-
blah-blah-blah-blah-
blah-blah-blah-blah-

blah-blah-blah-blah-
blah-blah-blah-blah-
blah-blah-blah-blah-
blah-blah-blah-blah-

(The device was now fully assembled. It looked beautiful and ridiculous and positively antediluvian.)

blah-blah-blah-blah-
blah-blah-blah-blah-
blah-blah-blah-blah-
blah-blah-blah-blah-
blah-blah-blah-blah-
blah-blah-blah-blah-
blah-blah-blah-blah-
blah-blah-blah-blah-
blah-blah-blah-blah-
blah-blah-blah-blah-
blah-blah-blah-blah-
blah-blah-blah-blah-
blah-blah-blah-blah-
blah-blah-blah-blah-
blah-blah-blah-blah-
blah-blah-blah-blah-
blah-blah-blah-blah-

(Just before I could ask how it worked, she sighed.)

blah-blah-blah-blah-

blah-blah-blah-blah-
blah-blah-blah-blah-
blah-blah-blah-blah-
blah-blah-blah-blah-

("Such a good man he was. I thank the Lord every day for having put that man in my way. He took him away from me after twenty-two years of bliss, but even if I had to go through that pain ten times over, those twenty-two years would still be worth it.")

blah-blah-blah-blah-
blah-blah-blah-blah-
blah-blah-blah-blah-
blah-blah-blah-blah-
blah-blah-blah-blah-
blah-blah-blah-blah-
blah-blah-blah-blah-
blah-blah-blah-blah-
blah-blah-blah-blah-
blah-blah-blah-blah-
blah-blah-blah-blah-
blah-blah-blah-blah-
blah-blah-blah-blah-
blah-blah-blah-blah-
blah-blah-blah-blah-
blah-blah-blah-blah-
blah-blah-blah-blah-
blah-blah-blah-blah-

blah-blah-blah-blah-
blah-blah-blah-blah-
blah-blah-blah-blah-
blah-blah-blah-blah-
blah-blah-blah-blah-
blah-blah-blah-blah-
blah-blah-blah-blah-
blah-blah-blah-blah-
blah-blah-blah-blah-
blah-blah-blah-blah-
blah-blah-blah-blah-
blah-blah-blah-blah-
blah-blah-blah-blah-
blah-blah-blah-blah-
blah-blah-blah-blah-
blah-blah-blah-blah-
blah-blah-blah-blah-

(This was not the first time I was hearing about my holy grandfather. His death by cancer of the pancreas had ensured his immortality in my grandmother's cosmology. The indulgence of her memory neatly obliterated what flaws—if any—he had had. Since I can remember, this man has been held up to me as the very font of goodness. He was a kind and considerate man, a devoted husband, a good father, an excellent doctor, a man of wit and culture, a lover of music and nature; he was wise, thoughtful, sensible, wary, rational, discreet, judicious, cool, sober, staid, well behaved, modest, steady, virtuous; he was

exempt from the common sins of envy, laziness, drink,
lechery, tardiness; he was never known to be evil-tempered,
pompous, smug, capricious, rude, insolent; and he was the
possessor—it was a beacon, a lighthouse of his goodness—of
magical blue eyes of which mine were only washed-out,
watered-down imitations.)

blah-blah-blah-blah-
blah-blah-blah-blah-
blah-blah-blah-blah-
blah-blah-blah-blah-
blah-blah-blah-blah-
blah-blah-blah-blah-
blah-blah-blah-blah-
blah-blah-blah-blah-
blah-blah-blah-blah-
blah-blah-blah-blah-
blah-blah-blah-blah-
blah-blah-blah-blah-
blah-blah-blah-blah-
blah-blah-blah-blah-
blah-blah-blah-blah-

(For me, the man exists only in black-and-white pho-
tographs, so I cannot verify any of his attributes myself, not
even the blueness of his eyes. He is a short, slightly plump
man with a balding head and a perfectly oval face. He has a
tiny moustache. He is neither handsome nor ugly. He only
looks out fixedly and mysteriously. I have often tried to

*extract a personality from these prints, to imagine the man
beyond the frozen frames. He does indeed look like a kind
man; perhaps a kind man of no ambition, amply content to
live his life out quietly with his family. Inoffensive, maybe
even bland. But solid. And with a quiet voice, I'd think.)*

blah-blah-blah-blah-
blah-blah-blah-blah-
blah-blah-blah-blah-
blah-blah-blah-blah-
blah-blah-blah-blah-
blah-blah-blah-blah-
blah-blah-blah-blah-
blah-blah-blah-blah-
blah-blah-blah-blah-
blah-blah-blah-blah-
blah-blah-blah-blah-
blah-blah-blah-blah-
blah-blah-blah-blah-
blah-blah-blah-blah-
blah-blah-blah-blah-
blah-blah-blah-blah-
blah-blah-blah-blah-
blah-blah-blah-blah-
blah-blah-blah-blah-
blah-blah-blah-blah-
blah-blah-blah-blah-
blah-blah-blah-blah-

blah-blah-blah-blah-
blah-blah-blah-blah-
blah-blah-blah-blah-
blah-blah-blah-blah-
blah-blah-blah-blah-
blah-blah-blah-blah-
blah-blah-blah-blah-
blah-blah-blah-blah-
blah-blah-blah-blah-
blah-blah-blah-blah-
blah-blah-blah-blah-
blah-blah-blah-blah-

(*"So how does it work?"* I *put in, taking advantage of a pause.*

"It runs on memories."

"Sorry?"

"I said, It runs on memories."

She suffered a sudden fit of coquetry and started arranging her hair with her fingers. She cleared her throat.)

blah-blah-blah-blah-
blah-blah-blah-blah-
blah-blah-blah-blah-
blah-blah-blah-blah-
blah-blah-blah-blah-
blah-blah-blah-blah-
blah-blah-blah-blah-
blah-blah-blah-blah-

blah-blah-blah-blah-
blah-blah-blah-blah-
blah-blah-blah-blah-
blah-blah-blah-blah-

(Memories?)

blah-blah-blah-blah-
blah-blah-blah-blah-
blah-blah-blah-blah-
blah-blah-blah-blah-
blah-blah-blah-blah-
blah-blah-blah-blah-
blah-blah-blah-blah-
blah-blah-blah-blah-
blah-blah-blah-blah-
blah-blah-blah-blah-
blah-blah-blah-blah-
blah-blah-blah-blah-

(She brought her mouth close the horn. "I," she said clearly, "I remember....")

blah-blah-blah-blah-
blah-blah-blah-blah-
blah-blah-blah-blah-
blah-blah-blah-blah-
blah-blah-blah-blah-
blah-blah-blah-blah-

blah-blah-blah-blah-
blah-blah-blah-blah-
blah-blah-blah-blah-

(A sharp click sound. Followed by the most bizarre little noise, a combination of a kettle whistling and a tiny locomotive starting up. And unmistakably coming from within the box.)

blah-blah-blah-blah-
blah-blah-blah-blah-
blah-blah-blah-blah-
blah-blah-blah-blah-
blah-blah-blah-blah-
blah-blah-blah-blah-
blah-blah-blah-blah-

("It still works!" she said, bringing her hands to her mouth. "Oh dear, oh dear.")

blah-blah-blah-blah-
blah-blah-blah-blah-
blah-blah-blah-blah-
blah-blah-blah-blah-
blah-blah-blah-blah-

(That's when she started.)

blah-blah-blah-blah-

blah-blah-blah-blah-
blah-blah-blah-blah-
blah-blah-blah-blah-
blah-blah-blah-blah-
blah-blah-blah-blah-
blah-blah-blah-blah-
blah-blah-blah-blah-
blah-blah-blah-blah-
blah-blah-blah-blah-
blah-blah-blah-blah-
blah-blah-blah-blah-
blah-blah-blah-blah-
blah-blah-blah-blah-
blah-blah-blah-blah-
blah-blah-blah-blah-
blah-blah-blah-blah-
blah-blah-blah-blah-
blah-blah-blah-blah-
blah-blah-blah-blah-
blah-blah-blah-blah-
blah-blah-blah-blah-
blah-blah-blah-blah-
blah-blah-blah-blah-
blah-blah-blah-blah-
blah-blah-blah-blah-
blah-blah-blah-blah-
blah-blah-blah-blah-
blah-blah-blah-blah-
blah-blah-blah-blah-
blah-blah-blah-blah-

blah-blah-blah-blah-
blah-blah-blah-blah-
blah-blah-blah-blah-

("I remember how I met my husband. My dear sweet hus-
band. I was sixteen and I was dressed in white. I was also
wearing a straw hat only it was too small and I was always
losing it in the wind. This was....")

blah-blah-blah-the
last day before
returning home to
Lévis, he asked me
whether he could write
to me and would I
answer back. I've kept
all his letters. Thirty-
seven in a little over a
month. In the thirty-
seventh he informed
me that he was driving
down to ask for me in
marriage. He bought a
brand new suit just for
the occasion and he
washed and waxed his
car. He brought Father
Bouillon along for
moral support and as a

character witness for
my parents. It was a
Saturday in early
September. We agreed
to meet by the church. I
saw the car drive up
and I saw him step out
nervously. And while
Father Bouillon, who
didn't know how to
drive, drove around the
block, my husband, a
man of thirty but as shy
as I was, asked for my
hand. He wanted to
kiss me—and I
wouldn't have stopped
him—but there were
people walking by. I ran
all the way home and,
while a suitable hour
went by, I sat on my
bed, unable to read a
line in my book,
bursting with
happiness, that
wonderful Yes, Yes, Yes
resonating in my heart.
He came at exactly

four, my handsome
knight, and Father
Bouillon, who had
already mentioned
several times in glowing
terms this doctor friend
of his in his letters to
my parents, spoke far
too much for a priest
and all went well. Next
spring I was seventeen
and a doctor's wife, and
six months later I was a
woman. For six months
the good man didn't
touch me. For six
months. Such a
respectful, caring,
tender man. What luck
I had, what a blessing
he was. I could never
have found a better
man. I thank the Lord
every day for His gift.
I've had many men
propose to me since he
passed away, but no one
could replace my
sweetheart, no one. Oh

Lord, I have su-su-
suffered so much!

She's crying.

(Far from slowing down or stopping at this interruption, the machine, with a click and a clack, kicked into even higher gear.)

As he was dying, he
told me, "At least I die
knowing that our
children have a good
mother." I worked
myself to the bone to
bring them up so their
father would be proud
of them. It wasn't easy,
God knows. In those
days, a widow with four

children, it wasn't easy.
But I managed. I did
what I had to. And
their father would be
proud of them! They
are good children. They
made their sacrifices,
too. His example blah-
blah-blah-blah-blah-
blah-blah-blah-blah-
blah-blah-blah-blah-
blah-blah-blah-blah-
blah-blah-blah-blah-
blah-blah-blah-blah-
blah-blah-blah-blah-
blah-blah-blah-blah-
blah-blah-blah-blah-
blah-blah-blah-blah-
blah-blah-blah-blah-
blah-blah-blah-blah-
blah-blah-blah-blah-
blah-blah-blah-blah-
blah-blah-blah-blah-
blah-blah-blah-blah-
blah-blah-blah-blah-
blah-blah-blah-blah-
blah-blah-blah-blah-

blah-blah-blah-blah-
blah-blah-blah-blah-
blah-blah-blah-blah-
blah-blah-blah-blah-
blah-blah-blah-blah-
blah-blah-blah-blah-
blah-blah-blah-blah-
blah-blah-blah-blah-
blah-blah-blah-blah-
blah-blah-blah-blah-
blah-blah-blah-blah-
blah-blah-blah-blah-   This woman.
blah-blah-blah-blah-
blah-blah-blah-blah-
blah-blah-blah-blah-
blah-blah-blah-blah-
blah-blah-blah-blah-
blah-blah-blah-blah-
blah-blah-blah-blah-
blah-blah-blah-blah-
blah-blah-blah-blah-
blah-blah-blah-blah-
blah-blah-blah-blah-
blah-blah-blah-blah-
blah-blah-blah-blah-
blah-blah-blah-blah-
blah-blah-blah-blah-
blah-blah-blah-blah-
blah-blah-blah-blah-

blah-blah-blah-blah-
blah-blah-blah-blah-
blah-blah-blah-blah-
blah-blah-blah-blah-
blah-blah-blah-blah-
blah-blah-blah-blah-
blah-blah-blah-blah-
blah-blah-blah-blah-
blah-blah-blah-blah-
blah-blah-blah-blah-
blah-blah-blah-blah-
blah-blah-blah-blah-
blah-blah-blah-blah-
blah-blah-blah-blah-
blah-blah-blah-blah-
blah-blah-blah-blah-
blah-blah-blah-blah-
blah-blah-blah-blah-
blah-blah-blah-blah-
blah-blah-blah-blah-
blah-blah-blah-blah-
blah-blah-blah-blah-
blah-blah-blah-blah-
blah-blah-blah-blah-
blah-blah-blah-blah-
blah-blah-blah-blah-
blah-blah-blah-blah-

Soft, white, wrinkled face. Green eyes but red this moment. An exasperatingly familiar face that I have known since I can remember. With pouts, stares and glares that are beyond the description of words but that all of us in the family know all too well. A woman who has *always* been in my life.

But not for much longer, I suppose.

blah-blah-blah-blah-
blah-blah-blah-blah-
blah-blah-blah-blah-
blah-blah-blah-blah-
blah-blah-blah-blah-
blah-blah-blah-blah-
blah-blah-blah-blah-
blah-blah-blah-blah-
blah-blah-blah-blah-
blah-blah-blah-blah-
blah-blah-blah-blah-
blah-blah-blah-blah-
blah-blah-blah-blah-
blah-blah-blah-blah-
blah-blah-blah-blah-
blah-blah-blah-blah-
blah-blah-blah-blah-
blah-blah-blah-blah-
blah-blah-blah-blah-
blah-blah-blah-blah-
blah-blah-blah-blah-
blah-blah-blah-blah-
blah-blah-blah-blah-
blah-blah-blah-blah-
blah-blah-blah-blah-
blah-blah-blah-blah-
blah-blah-blah-blah-
blah-blah-blah-blah-
blah-blah-blah-blah-
blah-blah-blah-blah-

Then I will be a parallel
line without one of its
companion lines.

Sad.

blah-blah-blah-blah-
blah-blah-blah-blah-
blah-blah-blah-blah-
blah-blah-blah-blah-
blah-blah-blah-blah-
blah-blah-blah-blah-
blah-blah-blah-blah-
blah-blah-blah-blah-　　　　And what will be left
blah-blah-blah-blah-　　　　of her?
blah-blah-blah-blah-
blah-blah-blah-blah-
blah-blah-blah-blah-
blah-blah-blah-blah-
blah-blah-blah-blah-
blah-blah-blah-blah-
blah-blah-blah-blah-
blah-blah-blah-blah-
blah-blah-blah-blah-
blah-blah-blah-blah-
blah-blah-blah-blah-
blah-blah-blah-blah-
blah-blah-blah-blah-
blah-blah-blah-blah-
blah-blah-blah-blah-
blah-blah-blah-blah-
blah-blah-blah-blah-
blah-blah-blah-blah-
blah-blah-blah-blah-

blah-blah-blah-blah-
blah-blah-blah-blah-
blah-blah-blah-blah-   Her *things*. This cacoph-
blah-blah-blah-blah-   ony of matter, this suffo-
blah-blah-blah-blah-   cation. I hate all her junk.
blah-blah-blah-blah-
blah-blah-blah-blah-
blah-blah-blah-blah-
blah-blah-blah-blah-
blah-blah-blah-blah-
blah-blah-blah-blah-
blah-blah will you, my
child?   Eh?

Sorry.

I said, Get me the
photo albums, please.

Oh.

*(They are in a bookshelf near the piano. Volume after vol-
ume. The oldest ones have wooden covers bound with string
and pages of soft, heavy black paper; the others are the stan-
dard modern type, with pages full of scientific friction. I
brought over five volumes.)*

Thank you. Let's see....
There he is. My dear

sweetheart. This is
blah-blah-blah-blah-

*(Pictures of the mystery man. A medical-school graduation
portrait.)*

blah-blah-blah-blah-
blah-blah-blah-blah-
blah-blah-blah-blah-
blah-blah-blah-blah-
blah-blah-blah-blah-
blah-blah-blah-blah-
blah-blah-blah-blah-
blah-blah-blah-blah-
blah-blah-blah-blah-
blah-blah-blah-blah-   Yet wasn't I the boy who
blah-blah-blah-blah-   was in love with a teacup?
blah-blah-blah-blah-

*(Sitting at the dining-room table in this house, looking at
the camera.)*

blah-blah-blah-blah-
blah-blah-blah-blah-
blah-blah-blah-blah-
blah-blah-blah-blah-
blah-blah-blah-blah-
blah-blah-blah-blah-
blah-blah-blah-blah-

blah-blah-blah-blah-
blah-blah-blah-blah-
blah-blah-blah-blah-
blah-blah-blah-blah-   I remember this teacup. I
blah-blah-blah-blah-   was ten when I first set
blah-blah-blah-blah-   eyes on it. Even now I
blah-blah-blah-blah-   cannot visit Paris without
blah-blah-blah-blah-   seeking it out.
blah-blah **Now here**

(On a path in a wood, a cane in his right hand.)

blah-blah-blah-blah-
blah-blah-blah-blah-
blah-blah-blah-blah-
blah-blah-blah-blah-
blah-blah-blah-blah-
blah-blah-blah-blah-
blah-blah-blah-blah-
blah-blah-blah-blah-
blah-blah-blah-blah-   It's a teacup in the Musée
blah-blah-blah-blah-   Guimet from the early
blah-blah-blah-blah-   days of Augustus the
blah-blah-blah-blah-   Strong's Royal Saxon
blah-blah-blah-blah-   Porcelain Factory in
blah-blah-blah-blah-   Meissen. It's the real
blah-blah-blah-blah-   thing: a porcelain teacup
blah-blah-blah-blah-   from the place where in
blah-blah-blah-blah-   1709 two alchemists,

blah-blah-blah-blah-
blah-blah-blah-blah-
blah-blah-blah-blah-
blah-blah-blah-blah-
blah-blah-blah-blah-
blah-blah-blah-blah-
blah-blah-blah-blah-
blah-blah-blah-blah-
blah-blah-blah-blah-
blah-blah-blah-blah-
blah-blah-blah-blah-
blah-blah-blah-blah-
blah-blah-blah-blah-
blah-blah-blah-blah-
blah-blah-blah-blah-
blah-blah-blah-blah-

Ehrenfried von Tshirnhaus and Johann Böttger, discovered the long-sought secret for making true, hard-paste porcelain, something that had baffled the West since the fourteenth century, when porcelain was first introduced into Europe from China.

(On the rocky shores of the St. Lawrence on a windy day.)

blah-blah-blah-blah-
blah-blah-blah-blah-
blah-blah-blah-blah-
blah-blah-blah-blah-
blah-blah-blah-blah-
blah-blah-blah-blah-
blah-blah-blah-blah-
blah-blah-blah-blah-
blah-blah-blah-blah-

This teacup is over two hundred and fifty years old. On the inside, it's a pure, glistening white. On

blah-blah-blah-blah-
blah-blah-blah-blah-
blah-blah-blah-blah-
blah-blah-blah-blah-
blah-blah-blah-blah-
blah-blah-blah-blah-
blah-blah-blah-blah-

the outside, over a rich vanilla-yellow background, there are flowers, leaves, four ants and a vividly coloured butterfly.

(At the stern of a rowboat. A young woman, my grand-mother, at the bow.)

blah-blah-blah-blah-
blah-blah-blah-blah-
blah-blah-blah-blah-
blah-blah-blah-blah-
blah-blah-blah-blah-
blah-blah-blah-blah-
blah-blah-blah-blah-
blah-blah-blah-blah-
blah-blah-blah-blah-
blah-blah-blah-blah-
blah-blah-blah-blah-
blah-blah-blah-blah-
blah-blah-blah-blah-
blah-blah-blah-blah-
blah-blah-blah-blah-
blah-blah-blah-blah-

This Meissen teacup is lovely beyond words. The colours, the lines, the design, are of a clarity, a neatness, that mesmerize me. My eyes lock onto this beauty and cannot divert themselves. I want to move away, I am tired of looking at this teacup,

blah-blah-blah-blah-
blah-blah-blah-blah-
blah-blah-blah-blah-
blah-blah-blah-blah-
blah-blah-blah-blah-
blah-blah-blah-blah-
blah-blah-blah-blah-
blah-blah-blah-blah-

but still I do not turn. I keep staring. It is beautiful, this teacup, it is so beautiful it *exhausts* me.

(Sitting in a garden chair, bare-chested, with his arms around two of his boys, one my father, a child of seven.)

blah-blah-blah-blah-
blah-blah-blah-blah-
blah-blah-blah-blah-
blah-blah-blah-blah-
blah-blah-blah-blah-
blah-blah-blah-blah-
blah-blah-blah-blah-
blah-blah-blah-blah-
blah-blah-blah-blah-
blah-blah-blah-blah-
blah-blah-blah-blah-
blah-blah-blah-blah-
blah-blah-blah-blah-
blah-blah-blah-blah-
blah-blah-blah-blah-
blah-blah-blah-blah-

I was the boy who was in love with a teacup. Then I was sent to boarding school.

blah-blah-blah-blah-
blah-blah-blah-blah-
blah-blah-blah-blah-

(With all his children, in front of a canvas tent.)

blah-blah-blah-blah-
blah-blah-blah-blah-
blah-blah-blah-blah-
blah-blah-blah-blah-
blah-blah-blah-blah-
blah-blah-blah-blah-
blah-blah-blah-blah-
blah-blah-blah-blah-
blah-blah-blah-blah-
blah-blah-blah-blah-
blah-blah-blah-blah-
blah-blah-blah-blah-
blah-blah-blah-blah-
blah-blah-blah-blah-
blah-blah-blah-blah-
blah-blah-blah-blah-
blah-blah-blah-blah-
blah-blah-blah-blah-
blah-blah-blah-blah-
blah-blah-blah-blah-
blah-blah-blah-blah-
blah-blah-blah-blah-

I was sixteen and at that time, in at least one respect, I was like all adolescents: I was a collector. The concept of ownership was both natural and pleasurable to me. If I saw something that I liked, I wanted it. If

blah-blah-blah-blah-
blah-blah-blah-blah-
blah-blah-blah-blah-
blah-blah-blah-blah-
blah-blah-blah-blah-
blah-blah-blah-blah-
blah-blah-blah-blah-
blah-blah-blah-blah-
blah-blah-blah-blah-

I didn't have it, I would work towards having it. If I had it and didn't care for it any more, I would store it. It seemed normal that much of the fun of my life should revolve around dry goods of varying sizes.

(Sitting in a sun-splashed landscape of snow, she with a radiant smile.)

blah-blah-blah-blah-
blah-blah-blah-blah-
blah-blah-blah-blah-
blah-blah-blah-blah-
blah-blah-blah-blah-
blah-blah-blah-blah-
blah-blah-blah-blah-
blah-blah-blah-blah-
blah-blah-blah-blah-
blah-blah-blah-blah-
blah-blah-blah-blah-
blah-blah-blah-blah-
blah-blah-blah-blah-
blah-blah-blah-blah-
blah-blah-blah-blah-

But at boarding school, due to some planner's mistaken faith in the confraternity of male adolescents, the doors to our rooms did not have locks. My possessions were exposed to every thief, prankster and enemy. And being a new boy at this boarding school, I happened to be

blah-blah-blah-blah-
blah-blah-blah-blah-
blah-blah-blah-blah-
blah-blah-blah-blah-
blah-blah-blah-blah-
blah-blah-blah-blah-
blah-blah-blah-blah-
blah-blah-blah-blah-
blah-blah-blah-blah-
blah-blah-blah-blah-
blah-blah-blah—oh,
this one!

assigned as a roommate a boy who didn't want a roommate, who wanted one of the few single rooms, a boy who was vicious and intelligent and without a single moral fibre in his body and whose friends inhabited the rooms around ours.

(A frontal portrait done some weeks before his death.)

blah-blah-blah-blah-
blah-blah-blah-blah-
blah-blah-blah-blah-
blah-blah-blah-blah-
blah-blah-blah-blah-
blah-blah-blah-blah-
blah-blah-blah-blah-
blah-blah-blah-blah-
blah-blah-blah-blah-
blah-blah-blah-blah-
blah-blah-blah-blah-
blah-blah-blah-blah-
blah-blah-blah-blah-

In a very short time, I seemed to be surrounded by nothing but thieves, pranksters and enemies. I had a magnificent United Nations flag, full size. It was ripped to pieces the size of handkerchiefs. I had a little wooden sculpture from Mauritius, a gift

blah-blah-blah-blah-
blah-blah-blah-blah-
blah-blah-blah-blah-
blah-blah-blah-blah-
blah-blah-blah-blah-
blah-blah-blah-blah-
blah-blah-blah-blah-
blah-blah-blah-blah-
blah-blah-blah-blah-
blah-blah-blah-blah-
blah-blah-blah-blah-
blah-blah-blah-blah-
blah-blah-blah-blah-
blah-blah-blah-blah-
blah-blah-blah-blah-
blah-blah-blah-blah-
blah-blah-blah-blah-
blah-blah-blah-blah-
blah-blah-blah-blah-
blah-blah-blah-blah-
blah-blah-blah-blah-
blah-blah-blah-blah-
blah-blah-blah-blah-
blah-blah-blah-blah-
blah-blah-blah-blah-
blah-blah-blah-blah-
blah-blah-blah-blah-

from my grandmother that I greatly valued. While I was sick in the infirmary with a fever once—three days of amazing peace—its legs were broken off and its body was glued to my desk. I had many books, paperback and hardcover, an eclectic but mainly historical collection. Some I never recovered, were plainly stolen; some I found with the covers ripped off, sad bodies of pages with yellow glue spines; others, the converse—it was the hollow covers I was left with. The pockets of my jackets were ripped off. My posters were mutilated. My calculator was stolen. The list goes on. All the objects silly and serious that constituted my intimate universe were attacked.

blah-blah-blah-blah-
blah-blah-blah-blah-
blah-blah-blah-blah-
blah-blah-blah-blah-
blah-blah-blah-blah-
blah-blah-blah-blah-
blah-blah-blah-blah-
blah-blah-blah-blah-
blah-blah-blah-blah-
blah-blah-blah-blah-
blah-blah-blah-blah-
blah-blah-blah-blah-
blah-blah-blah-blah-
blah-blah-blah-blah-
blah-blah-blah-blah-
blah-blah-blah-blah-

Each time I discovered
that something of mine
was gone or destroyed, I
felt a pain akin to a
physical pain. At the time,
you see, my nerve system
extended from my body
to all these objects. They
were not just mine—they
were *me*.

*(Reclining in any easy chair, covered with a blanket, asleep;
the beginning of his illness?)*

blah-blah-blah-blah-
blah-blah-blah-blah-
blah-blah-blah-blah-
blah-blah-blah-blah-
blah-blah-blah-blah-
blah-blah-blah-blah-
blah-blah-blah-blah-
blah-blah-blah-blah-
blah-blah-blah-blah-

I tried to cope. I tried
protection. But no matter
how good the locks I
installed on my desk, I
would return to my room

blah-blah-blah-blah-
blah-blah-blah-blah-
blah-blah-blah-blah-
blah-blah-blah-blah-
blah-blah-blah-blah-
blah-blah-blah-blah-
blah-blah-blah-blah-
blah-blah-blah-blah-
blah-blah-blah-blah-
blah-blah-blah-blah-

to find them ripped out and the contents of my drawers strewn all over the place. I tried concealment. This only increased the malice with which my valuables were destroyed once they were found out.

(Looking out from underneath a blanket at a child of no more than five years, my aunt, who is looking at him, puzzled.)

blah-blah-blah-blah-
blah-blah-blah-blah-
blah-blah-blah-blah-
blah-blah-blah-blah-
blah-blah-blah-blah-
blah-blah-blah-blah-
blah-blah-blah-blah-
blah-blah-blah-blah-
blah-blah-blah-blah-
blah-blah-blah-blah-
blah-blah-blah-blah-
blah-blah-blah-blah-
blah-blah-blah-blah-

There was nothing to be done. I was helplessly open to hurt.

blah-blah-blah-blah-

(Sitting on a bench, looking away.)

blah-blah-blah-blah-
blah-blah-blah-blah-
blah-blah-blah-blah-
blah-blah-blah-blah-
blah-blah-blah-blah-
blah-blah-blah-blah-
blah-blah-blah-blah-
blah-blah-blah-blah-
blah-blah-blah-blah-
blah-blah-blah-blah-
blah-blah-blah-blah-
blah-blah-blah-blah-
blah-blah-blah-blah-
blah-blah-blah-blah-
blah-blah-blah-blah-
blah-blah-blah-blah-
blah-blah-blah-blah-
blah-blah-blah-blah-
blah-blah-blah-blah-
blah-blah-blah-blah-
blah-blah-blah-blah-
blah-blah-blah-blah-
blah-blah-blah-blah-

Sometime then, I dimly perceived that there was an alternative to protection: poverty. If I didn't own anything, then I couldn't be hurt through what I owned. A ripped flag, a torn poster, a desecrated book wouldn't hurt me if I didn't own a flag, a poster, a book. That's how I started the process of retracting my nerve endings. At first I made a virtue of necessity. I tolerated the destruction of my outer

222

blah-blah-blah-blah-
blah-blah-blah-blah-
blah-blah-blah-blah-
blah-blah-blah-blah-
blah-blah-blah-blah-
blah-blah-blah-blah-

manifestations simply to
survive my boarding-
school days.

(Group photo. Second from left.)

blah-blah-blah-blah-
blah-blah-blah-blah-
blah-blah-blah-blah-
blah-blah-blah-blah-
blah-blah-blah-blah-
blah-blah-blah-blah-
blah-blah-blah-blah-
blah-blah-blah-blah-
blah-blah-blah-blah-
blah-blah-blah-blah-
blah-blah-blah-blah-
blah-blah-blah-blah-
blah-blah-blah-blah-
blah-blah-blah-blah-
blah-blah-blah-blah-
blah-blah-blah-blah-
blah-blah-blah-blah-

I suppose that after
boarding school, once I
was in the gentle real
world where locks are
considered something
normal, I could have
returned to my old ways.
But some latent
inclination made me
pursue my questioning.
What did that word
"ownership" mean

blah-blah-blah-blah-
blah-blah-blah-blah-
blah-blah-blah-blah-
blah-blah-blah-blah-
blah-blah-blah-blah-
blah-blah-blah-blah-
blah-blah-blah-blah-
blah-blah-blah-blah-
blah-blah-blah-blah-
blah-blah-blah-blah-
blah-blah-blah-blah-
blah-blah-blah-blah-
blah-blah-blah-blah-

exactly? What did it imply? All around me I could see people's hunger for commodities, as if happiness were a bulk product. Was this right? Was this owning of so much really so necessary? Wasn't materialism perhaps nothing but a deception? A time-filler till death?

(Carrying an uncle or two on his shoulders.)

blah-blah-blah-blah-
blah-blah-blah-blah-
blah-blah-blah-blah-
blah-blah-blah-blah-
blah-blah-blah-blah-
blah-blah-blah-blah-
blah-blah-blah-blah-
blah-blah-blah-blah-
blah-blah-blah-blah-
blah-blah-blah-blah-
blah-blah-blah-blah-
blah-blah-blah-blah-
blah-blah-blah-blah-

Entire civilizations have organized themselves around objects. Columbus sailed the blue, Pizarro garroted Atahualpa, six million went into flames, Neil Armstrong kicked at the moon's dirt—all for the sake of teacups. But not me! I firmly decided that I would neither speak nor

blah-blah-blah-blah-
blah-blah-blah-blah-
blah-blah-blah-blah-
blah-blah-blah-blah-
blah-blah-blah-blah-
blah-blah-blah-blah-
blah-blah-blah-blah-
blah-blah-blah-blah-
blah-blah-blah-blah-
blah-blah-blah-blah-
blah-blah-blah-blah-
blah-blah-blah-blah-
blah-blah-blah-blah-
blah-blah-blah-blah-
blah-blah-blah-blah-
blah-blah-blah-blah-
blah-blah-blah-blah-
blah-blah-blah-blah-
blah-blah-blah-blah-
blah-blah-blah-blah-
blah-blah-blah-blah-
blah-blah-blah-blah-
blah-blah-blah-blah-
blah-blah-blah-blah-
blah-blah-blah-blah-
blah-blah-blah-blah-

exist through objects. I rooted out materialism from my way of living. It was ten years ago that I stopped endowing objects with meaning, ten years ago that I rechannelled this habit of appropriation. Now I am more preoccupied with furnishing my head than the place where I live. The most beautiful rooms I have entered have been empty ones. Warehouses full of light and dust. Empty attics with a view. Plains without trees. All rooms where my bare, fertile humanity has been most evident to me. I hope to be a pauper by the time I'm thirty. I want nothing but the human, nothing else.

(The last of the pictures. Full-length, standing, looking at

*the camera, background indistinct, hands in pockets of
jacket except for thumbs.)*

It *breaks* my heart that
such a good man
should have to die, *IT
BREAKS MY HEART!*

She's crying.

(Full throttle, actually trembling with activity.)

Poor woman.

Wh-why, dear Lord? Of
all people on this round
earth, why my

sweetheart? I don't doubt Your great, all-seeing wisdom, but why *my* sweetheart? I loved that man with all my being. I was happy with him for twenty-two years. For twenty-two years it was a pleasure to go to bed at night, it was a pleasure to wake up in the morning, it was a pleasure to go about my day. And then, then, this *unimaginable* ending. How did I survive? No. I died that day too. I will blah-blah-blah-blah-blah-blah-blah-blah-blah-blah-blah-blah-blah-blah-blah-blah-blah-blah-blah-blah-blah-blah-blah-blah-blah-blah-blah-blah-blah-blah-blah-blah-blah-blah-blah-blah-blah-blah-blah-blah-blah-blah-blah-blah-blah-blah-blah-blah-

But I find it so difficult to pull my eyes away from this Meissen teacup. It's trivial, laughably worthless, it's only a stupid little hot-liquid receptacle, a handicraft admixture of clays and paints—but did I mention how beautiful the butterfly is? Such

blah-blah-blah-blah-
blah-blah-blah-blah-
blah-blah-blah-blah-
blah-blah-blah-blah-
blah-blah-blah-blah-
blah-blah-blah-blah-
blah-blah-blah-blah-
blah-blah-blah-blah-
blah-blah-blah-blah-
blah-blah-blah-blah-
blah-blah-blah-blah-
blah-blah-blah-blah-
blah-blah-blah-blah-
blah-blah-blah-blah-
blah-blah-blah-blah-
blah-blah-blah-blah-
blah-blah-blah-blah-
blah-blah-blah-blah-
blah-blah-blah-blah-
blah-blah-blah-blah-
blah-blah-blah-blah-
blah-blah-blah-blah-
blah-blah-blah-blah-
blah-blah-blah-blah-
blah-blah-blah-blah-
blah-blah-blah-blah-
blah-blah-blah-blah-
blah-blah-blah-blah-
blah-blah-blah-blah-

clarity, such sparkle. I
look at this teacup and
afterwards I feel better. I
feel a new sense of marvel,
a new depth to things. I
go and I delight in
meeting people. But then
I feel it again, I cannot
but feel it in this North
America that I live in:
materialism is a heaviness,
a tragic distraction. All
the human potential that
it wastes! I see this waste
all about me. I don't want
the captivity of
ownership. My life will be
something tight,
something essential. I
want nothing but the
human, nothing else.

blah-blah-blah-blah-
blah-blah-blah-blah-
blah-blah-blah-blah-
blah-blah-blah-blah-
blah-blah-blah-blah-
blah-blah-blah-blah-
blah-blah-blah-blah-
blah-blah-blah-blah-
blah-blah-blah-blah-
blah-blah-blah-blah-
blah-blah-blah-blah-
blah-blah-blah-blah-
blah-blah-blah-blah-
blah-blah-blah-blah-
blah-blah-blah-blah-
blah-blah-blah-blah-
blah-blah-blah-blah-
blah-blah-blah-blah-
blah-blah-blah-blah-
blah-blah-blah-blah-
blah-blah-blah-blah-
blah-blah-blah-blah-
blah-blah-blah-blah-
blah-blah-blah-blah-
blah-blah-blah-blah-
blah-blah-blah-blah-
blah-blah-blah-blah-
blah-blah-blah-blah-
blah-blah-blah-blah-

But who am I kidding? When my grandmother tends to her antique vacuum cleaner she is tending to only one thing: a long-lost man. Her possessions are intermediaries with the deceased eternal. They are the dregs of a cup of love that broke. They are not

blah-blah-blah-blah-
blah-blah-blah-blah-
blah-blah-blah-blah-
blah-blah-blah-blah-
blah-blah-blah-blah-
blah-blah-blah-blah-
blah-blah-blah-blah-
blah-blah-blah-blah-
blah-blah-blah-blah-
blah-blah-blah-blah-
blah-blah-blah-blah-
blah-blah-blah-blah-
blah-blah-blah-blah-
blah-blah-blah-blah-
blah-blah-blah-blah-
blah-blah-blah-blah-
blah-blah-blah-blah-
blah-blah-blah-blah-
blah-blah-blah-blah-
blah-blah-blah-blah-
blah-blah-blah-blah-
blah-blah. THE END.

made of what they are—
be it wood, plastic or
plaster—but of layer
upon layer of her sweat
and tears. They are
delicate shells of life.
Careful, Byzantine
exfoliations. Though
some may bear brand-
names, all are quite
unique, for they have
known her consideration.
Hoover, dishrag, Corning,
Sealomatic—these are the
family names of objects
that all have the same first
name. Doctor Emile
Hoover, Doctor Emile
dishrag, Doctor Emile
Corning, Doctor Emile
Sealomatic. The man is
still here, he has never left
this—eh!?

(The ending was abrupt. She shouted her last two words. The machine stopped with a sharp click and a low, blowing sound started.

"Is that it?" I asked.

"It should be long enough," she replied.

There was a high-pitched, grinding squeal. After a minute or so, it stopped. I heard a rolling metallic sound. Something was pushed through the machine's red velvet lips and plopped onto the table.

My eyes beheld a small elliptical mirror.

"There we go," said my grandmother. She held it up and looked at herself, satisfied. "Good. No blemishes. Sometimes, for larger mirrors, you get blemishes. And you have to talk forever longer and the pieces don't always fit together perfectly."

I took hold of the mirror. It was warm. The back was a grey, leaden colour. I looked at my reflection.

I looked closely.

Closer still, straining my eyes.

Lines of print. The silver surface of the mirror was made of layer upon layer of lines of print, neatly criss-crossing at right angles.)

(*I'm somewhat of an expert on the subject now. There are generally two places in old mirrors where it is possible, with the help of a magnifying glass, to detect the lines of print: on the very edges, where the silver is thinnest; and, especially, in the stains, where the oxidation sometimes brings out the print. Twice I have even managed to decipher words. The first time was in a New York objets d'art store. I was able to tell the storekeeper that a simple but pleasing antique hand-mirror was the work of a German. In the middle of a stain I had made out the words "ganz allein". The second time was on a subsequent visit to my grandmother. On the edge of her bedroom mirror I was able to read the syllables "ortneuf". I had no idea what word they came from until I asked her. "St-Raymond-de-Portneuf," she replied. This is how I found out where my grandfather was born. She added something that struck me: he was born nine months after his father died. If a moment of passion long ago had been delayed or interrupted by so much as a few days, I might never have been.*

Modern mirrors are of no interest. They are indeed industrially manufactured—and clear, totally clear. There's nothing to be seen in them.)

(She gave me the mirror. I still have difficulty with owner-ship—the apartment where I live is bare, I have few clothes, I own very little—but this pocket mirror is my one valuable possession. I look at it, and I try to imagine the words that I so stupidly ignored.)